THE
HELL'S
KITCHEN
CONNECTION

THE HELL'S KITCHEN CONNECTION
A Novel of Suspense

by
Robert B. Gillespie

DODD, MEAD & COMPANY   NEW YORK

Copyright © 1987 by Robert B. Gillespie
All rights reserved
No part of this book may be reproduced in any form
without permission in writing from the publisher.
Published by Dodd, Mead & Company, Inc.
71 Fifth Avenue, New York, N.Y. 10003
Distributed in Canada by
McClelland and Stewart Limited, Toronto
Manufactured in the United States of America
First Edition

1 2 3 4 5 6 7 8 9 10

Library of Congress Cataloging-in-Publication Data

Gillespie, Robert, 1938-
   The Hell's Kitchen connection.

   I. Title.
PS3557.I3795H45   1987   813'.54   86-24278

ISBN 0-396-08883-X

*To the same old seven faces,
Especially the one who's gone.*

Also by Robert B. Gillespie

**EMPRESS OF CONEY ISLAND
HEADS YOU LOSE
PRINT-OUT**

THE HELL'S KITCHEN CONNECTION

1

The fright came later. At the moment that the first attempt was made on Tom Costigan's life, I was immobilized by the crazy unexpectedness of it—a live hand grenade dropping onto the carpeted floor between Costigan and myself. My first fuzzy thought was that it was a joke concocted by one of the cartoonists. Their idea of humor was quite primitive. The grenade hissed. I half expected the infernal thing to pop open and wave a flag, saying, *"BANG!"* If it didn't, well, then all three of us were going to be blown to kingdom come bloody and disheveled. I stared at the grenade, unable to move.

We were in Alice Costigan's quarters on the top floor of Tom's house in Hell's Kitchen, a rough area on the West Side of Manhattan that had once been the bailiwick of an Irish gangster named Owney Madden. That was before the Mafia took over from the Irish and long before the blacks and Puerto Ricans came in to challenge the Italian rule. The Costigan house was built at the turn of the century, one of a row of modest town houses, many of which were now subdivided into squalid little habitats for rootless people. Alice's living area was once the servant's quarters, which she had converted into her sanctuary, her retreat from her father.

It was two days after Labor Day, one of the last simmering days of summer, and the side panes in the skylight over her sitting room were open. She had just come from the kitchen with a pitcher of iced tea and was about to place it on a side table when the grenade dropped from the skylight.

I speak of it as an attempt on Costigan's life because I felt like killing him myself at the time. But choking was what I had in mind, not mass slaughter. He was an abrasive man who took great delight in getting me angry. And every time he did it I vowed to stay away from him, knowing of course that I couldn't, for I was tied to him in two ways—I was his editor at the syndicate, and I was a close friend of his daughter.

She was the reason I was there that night.

We had been to a protest meeting at the local church hall. St. James the Less was a prisonlike structure midblock on West Forty-fifth Street, the color of dirt, and the low-ceilinged dungeon beneath it served as its hall. What we were protesting was the city's megalomaniacal plan to transform the fabled Times Square area of New York City into another Rockefeller Center—replacing sleazy human vice with inhuman, high-rise icebergs—a project that would inevitably bring drastic change to Hell's Kitchen, which was attached to Times Square like an appendix. The change was called "gentrification."

I suppose you could label Hell's Kitchen a slum, because many of the buildings were old and grimy, and the rat population outnumbered the human. But, by God, it was a neighborhood as the uptight Upper East Side was not, a mixed neighborhood of many nationalities who got along tolerably well. The church bound the Irish and Italians together, married them, as a matter of fact, for better or worse; the neighbors knew each other, shopped at the same markets, shared their gossip and concerns. But the seeds of its doom lay in its location just a few steps west of midtown Manhattan. Developers don't give a hoot in hell about neighborhoods; they buy up, knock down, raise rents to impossible heights, force residents out, and replace vegetable markets with pink boutiques, all in the name of progress and a twenty-percent return on investment. That was what the protest meeting was about.

I had another motive. The one block of Forty-second Street between Times Square and Eighth Avenue was unique in all the cities of the world. It was tawdry, corrupt, depraved, filled with blatant sex of all varieties, crappy souvenir shops, and dank arcades. But it throbbed with life and was populated by creatures who didn't exist anywhere else. It was a freak show of gaudy streetwalkers and grotesque hawkers, assorted drunks, crazies, and lowlifes. . . . My point is that only there were they accepted by their peers and thus able to live out their peculiar lives in some semblance of dignity.

Everyone at the meeting agreed with this phase of the city's plan, the blotting out of this one-block blight and its replacement with something else. Even Alice Costigan and her father felt that the sinful street should be redeemed, by annihilation if necessary. I loved it as is. I was tall enough—six two—and hefty enough, though some of the heft was blubber, to discourage any hands-on approach to me; and with my shaggy, reddish-blond whiskers and unruly mop of hair, I could stroll the sidewalk without hindrance, appearing indeed at first glance to be one of the regular denizens. I liked the vitality of it all; I liked the idea that these people had a place of their own where they could be themselves without conforming. And although no one agreed with me, I thought the street was a necessary barrier that deterred the developers from crossing into our neighborhood.

I didn't speak of this at the meeting. I dislike shocking people. More than that, if I had spoken my thoughts I would have scandalized them, for many of them knew I was an ex-seminarian: I would have been tabbed some kind of a voyeur, which I suppose I was, and some kind of pervert, which I maintain I wasn't. I contented myself with shouting, "Hear! Hear!" and applauding and stamping my feet.

Tom Costigan spoke, barking his words as usual, of tying the city up in lawsuits until Hell's Kitchen freezes over. He was one of the few property owners at the meeting—most of the others were tenants—and I grudgingly set down to his credit that he was strong in his opposition to the plan even though the gentrification process would triple the value of his building. He was born in the house fifty-eight years ago and returned to it when his parents died. It was his roots, and the small backyard with the grubby ailanthus his ancestral soil, though he seldom stepped into it. Knowing it was there was enough.

He was an imposing man with an aura of barely restrained violence. He was the same height as his daughter, five eleven, but thickly muscled. When I dreamed of choking him, his neck in my hands was as full and unyielding as an unripe watermelon. His coloration was "black Irish," his hair dark and bristly, his face broad, his nose pugged. His rough-and-tumble was verbal, not physical, however, and this former prosecutor, who could make Mafia dons tremble in the docks, was as immobilized by the grenade at his feet as I was. He glared at it, as if to quell it through intimidation.

At the meeting, he said, "When the mayor chases the prostitutes and muggers out of Times Square, where are these creeps going to go? They're going to come here! They're going to infest our neighborhood and bring the rot with them. . . . I remember when Times Square was a place you could bring your family, when Frank Sinatra sang at the Paramount and the bobby-soxers lined up for miles . . ." Tom Costigan went on and on, and the audience applauded.

I went outside for a smoke, and Father Frank Garvin followed me out. He was a fidgety, fluttery sort of a man, graceful rather than effeminate, who never got the hang of masculine gestures; a gaunt man with a beak made more pronounced by sunken cheeks, and pale-blue eyes that never met mine but gazed at my shoulder instead.

I leaned my rear end against the wrought-iron fence and offered him a cigarette. His hand reached for it, hovered a moment as if sniffing the proffered object, then with a birdlike peck snatched it from the pack.

"I really shouldn't," he said in a soft tenor voice.

"I know. I'm going to give them up myself one of these days," I said.

His breath smelled of Listerine and alcohol. Not the sweet scent of sacramental wine. Raw whiskey. Booze. I lit the cigarette for him with my lighter. A wisp of breeze came up from the Hudson and disappeared.

"It gets hot down there," he said. "I mean, when a lot of people are there . . . and with the lack of ventilation, it's—"

"I know, Father," I said. "It's your way of showing us what hell is like."

"Oh, no," he protested. "It's not done deliberately. We wouldn't—"

"Just joking," I said.

He was a simpleminded soul, a perennial innocent with wits addled by alcohol. He asked if I kept up with any of my seminary classmates. He had gone to the same seminary as I had on Long Island, but I figured he was about twenty years before my time, which would make him about fifty-five years old. I knew what he was leading up to; he was a pest, but I liked him just the same.

"Afraid not," I said in answer to his question. "They're too busy tending to their flocks."

He was silent for a minute. Then he said, "Would it be all right if I dropped by to see you tonight, Edward?"

"Any time," I said. "You're always welcome, but not tonight. I'll be seeing Alice Costigan home, and I'll be late. How about tomorrow night?"

"Yes, that'll be fine," he said. "An evening like this raises the thirst, doesn't it?"

"Make it tomorrow night," I said.

5

* * *

After the meeting, I tried to steer Alice out for a quick getaway, but her father had gotten into an argument with the Democratic political leader, Hugh Mullen, a round and ruddy man who was every bit as pugnacious as Costigan. Alice was dutifully trying to pull her father away, and failing.

"Joey and I aren't talking," Costigan said to Mullen. "And that's that."

"Then I'll talk to him. Damn it, Tom, we need all the help we can get."

"Not from the Mafia we don't!"

The shorter man seemed to pat the air in front of Costigan soothingly. "Who says Joey Gargano is Mafia? He's a legitimate businessman, clean as a dog's tooth—"

"The dog has rotten teeth!"

"Okay, we won't go into that. The important thing is he's got connections, Tom, powerful connections—"

"Don't tell me about Gargano, Hughie. Didn't I grow up with him? Didn't we swim bareass in the river? Wasn't he my best man when I married Veronica? Don't tell me about Joey Gargano."

"Sure, you know him. All I'm saying is you're the one who changed, not him. You shouldn't have written those things about him, Tom, you really shouldn't. They hurt him. On my sainted mother's grave, he's no more criminal than I am."

Tom Costigan stopped and grinned down at the perspiring face of the politician. They had been walking up the street toward Ninth Avenue as they talked, Alice and I disgustedly trailing behind them. We nearly bumped into them when they stopped.

"It's interesting that you should say that, Hughie," Costigan said. "Are you admitting to criminal activity?"

"My God, Tom, I couldn't get into the Mafia if I wanted to. I'd have to change my name to Mullino or something, and wave my hands when I talked, now wouldn't I? Where's your common sense, Tom?"

Costigan put his arm around Mullen's shoulder, and

they walked on. "I wasn't thinking of the Mafia, Hughie. There are other criminal conspiracies besides the Cosa Nostra."

"Name one! Name one!"

"You don't read my column," Costigan chided him with mock sadness. "Nearly every hyphenated group in the country has its criminal gang . . ."

We let them walk ahead.

I said to Alice, "Your father is old enough to find his own way home. Let's split.".

She said, "He's going to get into a fight. I know it, I just know it. He's all keyed up, and I'm the only one he'll listen to when he's like that." She patted my arm. "Why don't you go on home and let me handle it. I'll see you tomorrow night."

I stayed with her. Her voice had a husky, musky quality that enthralled me, like mellow music in the middle reaches of a cello. As I say, she was extremely tall for a woman, with an erect, dignified carriage, slim and unselfconsciously graceful. Her face can only be described as plain; she had the darkish coloring of her father, a long, straight nose, and a thin, no-nonsense mouth. Her beauty was in her eyes—deep brown, alert, amused, observant. There was a serenity about her that soothed me, and yet an ever-present vitality, both physical and intellectual, that stimulated me.

Costigan and Mullen turned onto Ninth Avenue. Only one hazard lay between us and the Costigan house, the next block over: Philbin's Irish Pub.

When we got to the corner, I muttered, "Shit, they're going in."

Alice said, "You go home, Eddie. I can handle him."

"You don't get rid of me that easy," I said. "You promised me some iced tea."

We followed them into Philbin's.

It was an ordinary neighborhood bar with the same dank, beery smell tinctured with disinfectant in the rear near the rest rooms, the same loud male voices punctuated now and then with female screeches of laughter that you find in all of them. Only here the decor was blatantly Hibernian. There was a rack of shillelaghs over the cash register and a photograph of Billy Philbin being lowered to kiss the Blarney Stone. A dropped ceiling with indirect lighting featured silhouettes of shamrocks of many sizes; and the murky brown walls were decked with Irish mementos, dusty photos of Dublin, big-eared Irish immigrants, the green Irish countryside, and a genealogical map of Ireland taken from the *Daily News*. It was one of my own hangouts before I started dating Alice a year ago, though I never felt that I fully belonged or was fully accepted. It was a place to go to fill an empty hour or two.

Some of the regulars were there, and I gave them a perfunctory wave. Frankly, I was sick and tired of the lot. There was only one who interested me, and I didn't want to look at her now, not when I was with Alice, because my interest in this one person was purely sexual, or rather, impurely sexual.

Alice touched her father's arm. "Fifteen minutes, Da," she said.

He looked at her with a scowl, then nodded.

Brendan Power was holding court near the end of the bar. He was the poet who wrote "The Ballad of Bobby Sands" six or seven years ago, which got him back on the lecture circuit after he had outlived his welcome there. He was a poseur, a tall, gangling, once-handsome man with flowing blond locks, alcohol-flushed face, and a budding potbelly. In my opinion, his poetry stunk, but when he recited it in his dramatically mellifluous voice and turned on his beamish grin, he melted the hearts of Irish-American females from coast to coast. If he had been born here instead of in Ireland, he'd have made one hell of a born-again preacher.

His consort when he was in New York was a person named Honor O'Toole. It was she who set my unsanctified innards in an uproar even when she was perched a bar-length away. She had the smiling face of a mischievous little girl and the radiant body of a sex goddess out of an adolescent's dream. This was surely distracting enough, but with her, communication was a contact sport. When you were with her, you were the most interesting person in the world, and she reacted by touching you in laughter or sympathy, by hugging your arm, by moving her hip against yours, her thigh against yours, as if constantly reestablishing rapport, seemingly unaware of the havoc she was causing in the susceptible male.

She greeted Costigan and hugged his arm, and my own arm tingled with the contact.

I groaned, and Alice said, "Honestly! I don't see what you see in her."

I said, "Who?"

"The blonde in the sweater with the plunging neckline."

"You just answered your own question," I said.

"But she's so obvious."

"Yes," I said.

Alice studied me with an amused expression. "I'm learning about men through you, Eddie my love," she said. "I take it that women like her are a perambulating occasion of sin for most men."

"I wouldn't say that."

"What would you say?"

"More like a movable feast."

Alice surprised me by laughing.

I suppose I should point out that Alice and I were not your ordinary pair of lovers. In fact, we weren't even lovers in the physical sense, not yet anyway, though the thought of taking her to bed had occasionally—frequently—crossed my mind. My early years of celibacy and withdrawal from the society of beckoning women left me with an unhealthy complex of uncertainties, fears, inhibitions, and hangups. I was a thirty-five-year-old teenager who covered his insecurities with jokes.

Alice was in her late twenties, and I was pretty sure she was equally inexperienced. You see, she had gone further than I had: she had entered a convent before her twentieth year and had actually become a full-fledged nun—and then had leaped over the wall. I can only imagine that her sexual problems were similar to my own. We never talked about it, not really. Maybe she had no problems at all, I don't know. Anyhow, there we were, the odd couple.

Billy Philbin, after serving Costigan and Mullen, moved down the bar to us. He was a beefy man with bristly gray hair cut short, arms as hairy and muscular as most men's legs, and a sad smile that lit his gray face like a candle in a window.

He said, "Don't see you in here very often, Miss Costigan. You give the place class."

"Thank you," she said. "I'm not much of a drinker, I'm afraid."

Alice ordered a soft drink, and I ordered a beer. I tried a joke, but he didn't think it was funny. I said, "I'll have that Irish beer. Kieran." He told me that Kirin was a Japanese beer. I settled for what was on tap. He gave me the pitying smile that a full-blooded Irishman gives one who is only half Irish.

Costigan's voice was rising. "I'm out to get all the bloodsucking bullyboys; I don't care what their nationalities are. I have a column coming up, kids, that'll knock your pants off. It hits awfully, awfully close to home."

Honor O'Toole bumped against him. "Not another one on poor Joey Gargano?"

"Maybe. Maybe not," Costigan said. "You'll have to read the column."

She bumped him again. "If something's going to knock my pants off, I want to know what it is. Maybe I'll enjoy it."

The men around her laughed.

Costigan said, "I can't tell you now, honey, but I want a ringside seat when you read it."

More laughter.

Honor pouted, then gazed down the bar at me. "Ed Carey will tell me," she said. "Won't you, Eddie?"

I didn't know what Costigan was talking about, but I put a hand over my mouth and said, "The seal of the confessional. An editor never tells."

Honor started toward me in her most seductive walk, all in good fun. To tell you the truth, she scared me, sort of the way roller coasters scare kids. If I were a girl, I would have screamed. She was coming at me with claws extended, like a female fiend at a slumber party. Oh God, she was going to tickle me!

Alice whispered, "Need help?"

"No. . . . Yes!"

Alice stood up, and I cowered behind her, pretending that I was only pretending. "It's an unfair fight, lady," Alice said. "You're too well armed for the poor, defenseless man. If you touch him, he'll grovel."

"Let him grovel," Honor said. "I mean to find out what Tommy Costigan says in his column."

"It's time for Tommy Costigan to go home," Alice said. "Come on, Da."

Honor stopped. "Da?"

Costigan had a mean grin on his face. "Out of the way, Alice honey," he said. "I want to see what she does to Eddie."

The two women faced each other, eye to eye. I could tell that Honor was angry at the intrusion of another woman into her act, and, knowing her crazy Irish temper, I was afraid of a scuffle. I had no doubt that Alice could take the soft-living sexpot—I had tussled with Alice on the beach and knew her strength—but it would entail a terrible loss of dignity, and I didn't want that to happen.

I straightened up and said, "I give up. Costigan's column isn't about Gargano, it's about all of you and your conspiracy to take over the country. For details, read the column."

It was another one of my dumb jokes, and I expected them all to groan and boo the way audiences do when Johnny Carson comes out with a clunker. But they didn't. They looked stunned.

Honor grimaced and backed away.

Costigan explained that his blockhead of an editor didn't know what was in the column because the column hadn't been written yet.

Brendan Power started composing a poem he called "Philbin's Revolt." "There he stood so brave and so cool,/ And by his side stood Honor O'Toole..."

Costigan finished his drink and started saying his good nights. "I have to run now. Alice is serving us her famous brew—iced tea!"

While the group at the other end of the bar were having fun with this announcement, I felt a slight poke in the back, and a low voice said, "Don't turn around. Just tell Costigan, tomorrow at twelve."

I half turned and glanced in the mirror behind the bar. The gunsel was sitting on a stool behind me, staring into his beer. I always thought of Danny Dunn as a gunsel because he looked and acted like Elisha Cook, Jr., in *The Maltese Falcon*. He was short and had the same sullen, shifty eyes, and I knew him to be a practicing thief. In fact, he had no other means of support, as far as I could make out.

Alice and I went out, and Costigan joined us on the sidewalk.

"That was a really stupid thing to say," he growled.

"Sorry, Tom, it was all I could think of."

"What did you have in mind when you said it?"

"Nothing."

He kept after me all the way to the house, which fortunately was just around the next corner.

Inside the front door, Alice said, "You don't really want any iced tea, do you, Da?"

"Certainly I do," he said. "I have this terrible thirst."

We trudged up the stairs past uninhabited floors with spacious rooms, any one of which would have made a better bedroom than her small room at the top. But Alice couldn't stand her father any more than I could, so she made her quarters as far away from him as possible. It was my theory that she entered the convent to get away from the overbearing man. That was when they lived in Virginia and Tom was playing the role of Uncle Sam's Angry Man in the Justice Department.

As it turned out, Alice was as headstrong as he was, and was not destined to stay long in an order demanding obedience and servility. Still, she toughed it out for several years because she had joined a teaching order, and she loved teaching little children. Then, when her mother died and her father seemed so lost—and her own discontent with the strictures of religious life had reached the intolerable stage—she left the convent to go live with him and serve as his housekeeper and hostess.

It was only a few months later that his ingrained orneriness caught up with him. Over the years, he had so alienated his fellow workers in the field of justice that they finally forced him to take early retirement. The move back to New York followed.

Alice said, "Neither one of you really wants iced tea, do you?"

We assured her that we did, both of us lying. I knew I should have written the night off and gone home. But I was still hoping for a few moments of serenity with Alice. Alone.

She went into the kitchen.

While she was there, Costigan started on me again. I knew he was spoiling for a fight, and yet I couldn't keep my mouth shut. I said, "The trouble with writing about someone like Gargano is that no paper outside New York City will run it."

His tone turned nasty. "How do you know that, sonny? You don't know that at all, do you? So why do you say it? That's a bad habit you have. It shows a sloppy mind, and I can't stand sloppy minds."

Alice said from the kitchen, "Cut it out, Da. If you want to browbeat someone, go downstairs."

"Browbeat?" Costigan cried. "Was I browbeating you, Ed?"

"Yes," I said.

Costigan swiveled his head toward the kitchen. "And stop calling me 'Da,'" he cried. "It sounds like baby talk!"

"Okay, Da."

Costigan made a face. "Ever since she saw that dumb play, she's been calling me that." He raised his voice. "It's disrespectful, that's what it is!"

Alice appeared in the doorway. "It's Irish for father. What's wrong with that?"

"It's how you say it, Alice. I know when you're being sarcastic."

"What do you want me to call you?"

"Anything. Anything but Da."

Alice nodded. "Okay, Pops."

I laughed, and he lit into me again. I imagined my fingers around his bull neck, tightening, squeezing. I tried to agree with everything he said, but then he would say something that really stung, and I would retort, whereupon he would leap on my retort and pick it apart. I couldn't win.

I heard a faint noise on the roof and looked up at the skylight. I was sitting on the sofa, and Costigan was in the easy chair opposite me. I had the impression that something moved and disappeared. Those damned pigeons again, I thought.

Alice came into the room carrying a pitcher of iced tea. "Knock it off, Pops," she said. "I want you both to have your drink, and go."

Thunk.

The grenade landed on the floor. The handle prevented it from rolling. It lay there for what seemed like a long period of time, but in reconstructing the incident later, I realized that it could not have been more than three seconds, assuming that it was designed to detonate in five from the moment it was activated. As I say, Costigan and I just sat there, mesmerized.

I heard Alice's exclamation, glimpsed her movement, saw her foot in a stop-motion blur as it whammed into the grenade soccer-style and sent it flying through the kitchen doorway. And immediately the flash, the ear-splitting blast, the concussion, the impression of fragments flying, the cloud of smoke and dust, and then the continuing sounds of cracking and crashing in the silence that followed. The cloud billowed out and enveloped us. I felt battered and dazed.

I peered dumbly at Alice. Her body was turned away from the blast and bent over the pitcher as if protecting it from contamination by the dust. I got to my feet and gripped her shoulder.

"Are you okay?" I managed to say. I wasn't sure whether I was supporting her or leaning on her.

She turned her head slightly to get me in sight. "That was a— That was a—"

I nodded. Then we both looked at Tom Costigan.

He was still in his chair, but now bunched tightly, as if ready to spring. The look on his face was terrifying—rage, outrage, billowing rage. I looked for blood on him, and there wasn't any.

He shot a glance at the skylight and said to us, "Stay here."

Just outside Alice's quarters, at the head of the staircase, was a metal-runged ladder to the roof. Costigan lumbered to it and started climbing.

Alice cried, "Da!" Then she turned to me. "Go with him. He'll be killed."

Utterly befogged, I started to follow, when my dust-clogged nose stopped me. "Gas," I said.

Costigan was making a racket in the darkness at the top of the ladder, thumping on the hatch cover and grinding out curses.

Another sound intruded. "My God, the water," Alice said.

She plopped the pitcher of tea on the side table, and we both rushed to the kitchen. A great spray of water was washing the dust from the air. Through it, we clambered over the jagged remnants of a wall cabinet and stumbled over shards of dishes, shattered containers of food, and large chunks of unspecified debris.

The shock of the water cleared my mind. I pointed

15

under the sink. "You get the water," I said. "I'll get the stove."

It wasn't that easy. The blast had moved the battered stove, but not far enough for me to get to the cutoff cock behind it. God bless the broken water pipes, I thought; the spray doused any fire before an explosive buildup of gas could occur. I manhandled the heavy monster until I could wedge my body behind it and find the break in the pipe. The gas was making me dizzy, and the damned stinking valve wouldn't budge when I tried to turn it. It probably hadn't been turned in decades.

"Wrench," I gasped to Alice, and miraculously she found one and snapped it into my hand like a nurse in an OR. I dropped it once and had to fish for it blindly, my nose right over the gushing gas. My desperate fumbling eventually succeeded, the valve turned without shearing off, and the flow of gas stopped.

Alice helped me out of the kitchen and sat me on the sofa. It was then that I noticed the shredded fabric and realized that fragments of the grenade had whistled within inches of my body and slashed the sofa in which I had been sitting.

It was then that the fright started.

2

I peered at Alice through a red haze and started laughing crazily. She had collapsed on the sofa beside me, thoroughly soaked, her eyes as large as a night creature's. To me, the sight of her was hilarious. Her black hair was plastered to her head; her thin dress clung to her like another skin. My laughing threatened to turn into hysteria, and I embraced her tightly.

"The gas," I said. "Laughing gas."

Alice pulled away. "My father," she said.

I held on to her. "He's all right," I said.

She stiffened in my arms. "Take a look," she ordered.

"Since you put it that way . . ." I said, groaning.

I relinquished her, made my way to the ladder, and climbed until my head projected over the lip of the hatchway. At first, I didn't see him. The roofs were approximately the same height, and I could see clear to the corner. Then I saw him—silhouetted like a large ape on a roof around the corner. He was yelling something, but I couldn't make out the words. He appeared to be beating his chest. No other creatures were in sight. I waited a moment to be sure, then descended.

"He's playing King Kong," I said to Alice, and told her what I had seen.

We collapsed once more on the sofa.

She said, "Someone tried to kill us."

I said, "It would appear so." That was my idea of dry humor. Understatement. I have a flip mouth, and it comes into play when things are most serious. It's a defense mechanism.

She said, "Someone put a bullet through our window when we lived in Virginia."

"What happened?"

"Nothing. We figured it was the Mafia. My father was prosecuting them at the time."

"They were just trying to scare him," I said.

"How do you know? It was a real bullet, Ed."

I let it go. I said, "All three of us could have been splattered on the wall."

"I know."

"If it weren't for your kick—"

"Lucky."

"Where'd you learn to kick like that?"

She yawned. "I played soccer at the academy. I was pretty good."

"Did you know it was a real grenade?"

"I don't know what I thought. It didn't belong there. I didn't want it there, and it seemed like a good idea to kick it the hell out of there, that's all."

"Good thinking," I said.

Costigan was back on his own roof. We heard him calling down to a neighbor.

"That was very kind of you to worry about us, Mrs. O'Malley. But you needn't have bothered. You see, I had some Boston baked beans for dinner, and I broke wind . . . I said I *farted*, so you see— No, it's kind of you to say so, but I don't think it was a record. I read somewhere that the San Francisco earthquake— Yes, I think you were right to call the police. Good night, Mrs. O'Malley."

We heard him mutter in a lower voice, "Nosy old bitch."

He slammed the hatch lid shut and clanged down the ladder. He stood in the doorway and glared at us.

"Are you two all right?" His question sounded like a growl.

We assured him that we were.

He said, "Alice honey, would you happen to know where I put my baseball bat?"

She said, "The police will be here in a minute."

"Where's the bat?"

"I haven't the foggiest. What do you want it for?"

"I'm going around and have a little talk with Joey Gargano."

"No, you're not," she said. "You're going to wait here for the police."

I said quickly, "I'll go down and wait for them at the front door." I stood up. It took me a minute to get my sea legs.

Costigan said, "He's at his table in Vinnie's. I told him I was coming, so he's waiting for me."

I couldn't help interrupting. "You were standing on Vinnie's roof and shouting. But you couldn't see whether Gargano was there or not."

"He's always there."

"And sometimes he comes over the roofs," I said, "and drops bombs through people's skylights, is that it?"

Costigan fixed me with a black look. "When he has something against them, yes."

"But it doesn't make sense, Tom," I said. "I thought gangsters were partial to silent bullets and cement shoes, not bombs that wake the whole neighborhood."

"You don't know your history of gang wars, sonny," he said roughly. "It had to be Gargano or one of his fish-eyed bullyboys.... God, why am I arguing with you! The hell with the bat; I'll take a poker!"

Alice stood up. "No, you won't."

"The one with the hook," her father said with murderous glee. "Don't you realize he tried to kill you, honey? My *daughter!* A poker up his fat ass ought to set him straight!"

He put his hands on her shoulders, and she shook them off.

I said, "I'll go down and wait for the police." I slipped past him and went down the stairs.

The police arrived in large numbers and overran the whole top floor and the roof. The bomb squad collected fragments, confirmed to us that what we had been assaulted with was indeed a hand grenade, probably of World War II vintage, and then departed in their strange beehive on wheels, just as the organized-crime force was arriving. The head of this group was a thin, jacketless, monkish-looking man named Fred Ferrante.

Having told our stories several times to succeeding groups of cops, we adjourned to Costigan's living room on the first floor. I sat by the air conditioner in the front window and shivered, trembled actually, my insides quivering with the false memory of fragments slashing through them, ripping, slicing, shredding, mashing.

Ferrante treated Costigan with the deference befitting the great crime fighter, but Costigan was being strangely reticent.

Ferrante said, "Yes, it looks like the bomb was directed at you, sir, but just to touch all bases—"

Alice stated, "I'm a schoolteacher," as if that dispelled any notion that she could have murderous enemies.

The policeman nodded gravely. "How about Mr. Carey?"

I gazed at him blankly, concentrating on what was happening in my stomach.

Costigan said, "Ed Carey is not the sort of person who makes enemies."

I wondered if he was insulting me. The words themselves weren't insulting; in fact, to a civilized person they were laudatory. But I knew Costigan, and what he was saying was that I was something less than a man. I smiled and said, "Same to you, Tom."

Costigan didn't mention Joey Gargano. Ferrante did.

"You've been giving Gargano a hard time," he said.

"Oh?" said Costigan.

"We read your column every week, sir. We find it very interesting."

"Glad to hear it, Inspector."

"Lieutenant," Ferrante said. "Do you think it was Gargano?"

"Have you seen him recently?" Costigan said. "He's gotten fat as a pig. Do you think he could climb over rooftops like that?"

"I understand he has a regular table at a restaurant called Vinnie's. That's right around the corner."

"I seem to have heard that," Costigan said.

Ferrante continued his respectful interrogation and got little useful information. Asking our own questions, we learned that the police found nothing important on the roof—no telltale matchpad, cigarette butt, or loose button clumsily dropped there by the skulking bomber. They had gone over the rooftops, testing doors and hatch covers to see if any were still unlocked, and had gone down fire escapes checking windows—all to no avail. They were now going door to door interviewing occupants. I assumed it was standard procedure and that they would come up empty.

My etymological brain was idly toying with the word *grenade* to keep from pondering more solemn subjects. The word derived from the Low Latin for pomegranate, a fruit known only to medieval poets, as far as I could make out. And yet, according to the history of gang wars, on which Costigan was such a damned expert, the gangsters of the Twenties called their grenades "pineapples." I supposed that the first hood who ventured to call them pomegranates would have been made to eat one. With grenadine . . .

In this manner, I coaxed my craven body out of its funk.

Alice had been able to change into dry clothes, but I was still sopping wet. I moved away from the air conditioner, and my trembling stopped. Of course!

Finally, Ferrante stopped asking questions and simply stared at Costigan. "You're playing a foolish game, Mr. Costigan," he said.

"I'm not exactly playing, Lieutenant," Costigan said.

Ferrante shook his head sadly, and a short time later left.

Costigan headed toward his fireplace.

"No poker," Alice said.

Costigan let his shoulders slump. "Maybe you're right," he said. "But I'm going to have a word with Gargano all the same."

I stood up and was about to say I was heading for home, when Alice said, "Very well, we're going with you."

I said, "Right."

Police vehicles still clogged the street, and neighbors stood in isolated clusters fixing their eyes on anything that moved. When Costigan appeared, they gravitated toward him. Several reporters. Flashbulbs. Costigan contemptuous.

"What happened?"

"We had a little explosion. No one was hurt."

"Who did it?"

"Some bomber or bombers unknown."

"Do you think it was the Mafia?"

"It's possible."

More questions were thrown at him, and Costigan fended them off. "The police know more about it than I do," he said.

Latecomers asked, "What happened?"

"We're redoing the top floor."

They pointed to me. "What happened to him?"

"He sweats easy," Costigan said.

They followed us around the corner onto Ninth Avenue, and when we entered Vinnie's Restaurant, they watched us through the front window.

The police were already there. Joey Gargano sat at his usual table in the rear, unflustered. Two policemen sat with him, one of them asking questions, the other taking notes.

Gargano was not grossly obese, just solidly and uniformly packed from top to bottom like a giant salami. Black hair neatly combed, dark complexion glistening from a half-century's intake of olive oil, the most striking thing about him were his eyes, which were large, black-brown pools of—what?—hell, sympathy, it's the only way I can describe them. The rest of his face was deadpan, but the eyes seemed to speak of love and kindness. Perhaps that was what made him so deadly.

He spotted Costigan coming toward him and said in his soft, gentle voice, "Are you all right, Tom? They've been telling me what happened." His hands remained on the red-checked tablecloth, one idly caressing a wineglass half-filled with Chianti.

Costigan stopped in front of the table. The two policemen stared up at him, unmoving.

"Was it you, Joey?" Costigan asked.

"No, Tom."

"One of your boys?"

Gargano shook his head gravely. "No."

Costigan switched his gaze to the policemen. "Was he here all the time?"

"That's what the owner says."

"Not even to go to the john?"

The one with the notebook said, "He went to the john twice, once at nine and once at ten-thirty."

"How long?"

"Five minutes. Maybe more, maybe less."

Costigan turned back to the quiet fat man. "You don't like my column."

"It's all right."

"What I said about you."

"You do what you have to do, Tom."

"I don't like anyone trying to smash my daughter."

"I understand."

"If someone's mad at me, leave my daughter out of it."

Gargano gazed at him with those great dark eyes.

Costigan said, "Anyone tries to blow me away better make damn sure he succeeds. Because if he doesn't—"

Alice interrupted him. "You've made your point, Da," she said. "Let's go."

Costigan's body relaxed. "Okay. See you around, Joey."

"See you around."

"How's Natalie?"

"Fine, fine."

"Good."

Without seeming to, Alice and I guided Costigan out the front door. He growled, "I still think I should've brought the poker." The neighbors half turned away from him, as if they just happened to be there.

He said, "I need a drink," and headed for Philbin's, three doors away.

I said to Alice, "Is he going to be all right?"

She sighed. "I suppose so."

"Where are you going to sleep?"

"In my own bed. That wasn't touched."

"You have new air-conditioning vents in the kitchen."

"It's a hot night."

I moved, and my shoes sloshed. The humidity must have been fierce, because I was no drier now than I had been two hours ago. I said, "What we need is a good hurricane."

"Not yet, please."

I said, "You're carrying your briefcase."

She looked down at the leather bag. "Force of habit," she said. "There are always papers to be corrected, and I can do it anywhere."

"Well." I shuffled my feet and sloshed. "I'm going home."

"You go on, or you'll catch your death."

"Are you going to bird-dog him home?"

"I suppose."

"Well." I gave her a chaste kiss. I wanted to do more, but we were on the avenue and I was all wet. "I guess the excitement's over for tonight."

"Go."

I watched her walk into Philbin's, erect, head high, her own special carriage not tilted to the left by the heavy briefcase. I almost went after her, but a momentary wave of bleariness suggested the wisdom of going home to my small apartment and going to bed.

I squished into my nest, shucked my sodden clothes, took a warm shower, poured a large whiskey on the rocks, sat in my imitation leather chair by the window, and pondered the enormity of what had happened. This lovable body of mine had come within a whisker of being an instant bloody corpse. I was still young enough to believe that my own death was in the far distant future, if it came at all. But tonight I came close to being called, and I had come apart, I had vibrated like a machine gone berserk. I envied the courage of Tom Costigan, damn his vicious heart. I envied his decisiveness, his—I hated to say it—his integrity.

He and Joey Gargano had grown up on the same block and had had the same religious training. But while Joey drifted into the protective arms of the Mafia, young Tom got in on the tail end of World War II as a naval ensign, flew through Stuyvesant Law School with the help of the GI Bill, and landed in the attorney general's office with the help of the local Democratic leader. This was long before Hugh Mullen's ascendancy. In Washington, his dogged aggressiveness and ability to think on his feet made him the ideal prosecutor. He had a form of tunnel vision, by which he could keep his eyes on the all but invisible thread of conspiracy in the uncharted maze of underworld double-talk, slippery alibis, irrelevancies, and dead-end diversions in months-long trials, and hold it up triumphantly for the jury to see. He put several dozen high-level hoods away, where a lesser prosecutor would have failed.

When he was untimely retired, he could have made himself a very wealthy man by moving to the other side of the courtroom, to the defendant's table. Instead, he came back to New York and wrote a book, called *Stranglehold*, about his experiences fighting the mob, which became a best-seller. I ghosted it. How I came to do that is another story.

The success of the book spurred whistle-blowers from all over the country to write to him about a wide variety of organized rackets that were strangling the American people. Some enclosed evidence in the form of documents, photos, tapes, and even physical objects such as guns, counterfeit money, ledger books, samples of soil, and even a severed finger.

And so Costigan continued his crusade against organized crime by writing a weekly column for the newspaper syndicate I worked for, the New York *Herald-Courier* syndicate. The column had the same title, "Stranglehold." I edited it, frequently rewrote it *in toto*, and, the laws of libel being what they were, I lawyered it in the first instance and, when he fought me, submitted it to the paper's lawyers for final adjudication. Being a lawyer himself, Costigan knew damn well what was libelous and what was not. But he fought me anyhow, just to give me a hard time. I think he disapproved of me as a potential son-in-law. In his eyes, no man was good enough for Alice, and certainly not I.

The whiskey wasn't doing the job. I lay in bed with my smarting eyes wide open. Someone had rammed home to me the fact of my fragile mortality. Who used hand grenades these days, for God's sake? The whole episode was unreal. In my mind, Alice said to me, "It was a real bullet, Ed." The Mafia doesn't fool around. That time in Virginia the bullet was a warning. If they had wanted to kill Costigan, they would have. This time the grenade was not a warning. It was meant to kill. But why Alice and me? Did they specifically want to kill us along with Costigan? Or were we innocent bystanders whom they didn't care about one way or another?

I got up and took a slug of Pepto-Bismol. My soul was filled with disquietude, which may or may not have been simply discontent with the less-than-dashing figure I had cut throughout the evening.

I went back to bed and did something I hadn't done in years. I said an act of contrition. "Oh my God, I am heartily sorry . . ."

My gritty eyes closed, and I was finally drifting to sleep. Then I remembered something. I had forgotten to give Costigan the message from the gunsel.

3

The next day it rained—a blustery rain brought on by a low-pressure area that had swung down from Canada. The man on the radio spoke of Hurricane Colleen that was threatening the east coast of Florida, a car bomb that killed nineteen Christians in Beirut, and a fire that killed a family of five in Canarsie. The news complemented my mood. I was in a deep state of melancholy, a rare occurrence with me. I was generally as buoyant and undepressible as my hero, Alfred E. Neuman, the *Mad* magazine mascot. This morning, I wrapped my gloom around me like a comforter rather than a hairshirt, and to tell the truth, I sort of enjoyed it.

I trudged crosstown to the office, which was on Forty-fourth east of Lexington, and enjoyed every slogging minute of it. I felt sorry for myself and liked the feeling. I was the mysterious hero of a Victorian novel hiding a tragic secret. The mood was shattered by my boss, Chuck Godbold, the director of the syndicate, who loomed in the doorway to my office.

"You look like a dead porcupine," he said. He was a bulky, blondish, balding man who cinched his belt tightly, as if it were a corset that would confine his corpulence, but instead only accentuated the bulges above and below. He was a man who expected to die before he was forty the way his father had, and was determined to live twice as vigorously as anyone else to cram eighty years of living into his allotted forty. He had recently attained that age, to his great surprise.

I said, "I was nearly blown up by a bomb thrower last night."

"You don't say," he said, not really listening. "Are we all set for the party?"

That was Chuck Godbold for you. Most people disliked him, but I had been with him for the better part of ten years, knew he could be a warmhearted sentimentalist on occasion, and I loved him. But don't take my word for it; I loved practically everybody.

One of the exceptions was J. P. Cosgrove, an arrogant and pompous bastard whom I detested. We were throwing a big bash to celebrate signing him for another year to produce his dreadful weekly column, "Take It From Me," which nobody read except me, who had to as his editor, and Horace Hawthorne, the idiot publisher of the *Herald-Courier*, who was thrilled to have such a distinguished author in his paper. Godbold had put me in charge of arranging the party at the Tom Jones Tavern, the glittering gyp joint on the edge of Central Park. The syndicate was losing a ton of money on the damn column, and the parent paper itself was on shaky financial ground, but old Horace doted on the famous novelist, and there was nothing Godbold or I could do to change his mind.

I said, "All set except the number of guests. The restaurant's been after me. They have to know."

Godbold promised to tell me by midmorning.

The syndicate offices were on the twelfth floor of the *Herald-Courier* building, and my work area was a glassed-in cubbyhole that shared a window with the larger cubbyhole of the assistant sales director next door. Outside was an expanse of open space that housed typists, copiers, shipping clerks, computers that transmitted columns to computers around the country, and small offset presses, all of which raised a din that was background noise to my valuable ruminations. This morning, my ruminations had a sabot in their machinery. The cogs weren't meshing.

The first thing that went wrong was the Cosgrove column. It was late to start with, and in the first paragraph he was referring contemptuously to a well-known author as a "faggot." Even in today's world, the paragraph was out-and-out libel.

As editor, I wasn't permitted to touch a word, not even a punctuation mark, in the column. After all, hadn't J. P. Cosgrove written a dozen long-winded, highly popular novels in the 1950s and 1960s that satirized the autocratic families of New England, delicately imputing to them all of the sins that cried to heaven for vengeance as well as some of the more engrossing mores of Sodom and Gomorrah? He was a stylist, by God, and a clumsy editor like myself could only louse it up. Never mind that the times had changed and nobody read his books anymore, nor, for that matter, his self-indulgent column of opinion. His list was down to twelve papers, some of which, I was sure, had simply forgotten to send in a cancellation.

I was in no shape to tussle with Cosgrove. I decided to let Chuck Godbold do it. I went down the row of cubbyholes to his office, only to be told by his secretary that he was at a meeting that could last all morning. The column couldn't wait; it had to go out immediately to a breathless public.

Cursing Cosgrove and Godbold in particular and the world in general as I went back to my office, I dialed Cosgrove's unlisted Manhattan number and got through Stanhope, the snooty butler, to the eminent author himself.

"Yes, Edward my boy?" he said. The condescending New England intonations made my back teeth tingle. I pictured the great lumpy face, the majestic tapir nose, the puffy rhinoceros eyes, and the sparse, slicked-back hair, and felt my stomach turn.

I stated as forcefully as I could what was wrong with the offensive paragraph. "There's no time to have it lawyered," I said. "But I can't send it out as it is, J. P."

"I don't see anything wrong with it," he said, speaking *ex cathedra*. "Send it out as written."

"But it's libelous on the face of it! We'll be sued for millions!"

"Nonsense. Truth is an absolute defense. Leave it alone, laddie."

I think I ground my teeth. "Truth is *not* an absolute defense," I said. "There's always the question of malice."

"Are you saying I wrote this maliciously?"

I refrained from telling him that everything he wrote dripped with malice. "I'm saying that what you've written is false, and it's libelous, and I can't send it out."

Cosgrove raised the question of burden of proof in a trial for libel. "Can't you just see him trying to prove that he's straight?" he said with a laugh that sounded like a gurgle.

"I think the burden would be on you, sir, to prove that he isn't," I said.

At length, after pounding me and belittling me for fifteen minutes, he said in a calm voice, "Very well, my craven editor, simply eliminate the whole first paragraph. You will notice that the rest of the column doesn't need it. I wrote it that way to see if you people were on your toes."

My second candidate for murder in two days! I saw that I would have to amend my self-image. Normally a person slopping over with the milk of human kindness, I now felt currents of malevolence I hadn't realized were there. I envisioned a hand grenade stuck up Cosgrove's cavernous nostril, hummed "Pop Goes the Weasel," and felt better.

Next came the Otto Walters column. I scarcely looked

at it. I knew it would be ponderously written, that it would carefully balance the arguments for (in this case, a nuclear moratorium) and the arguments against, and wind up with an appeal for wisdom. "The Great Explainer" he was known as, and as such was awarded a special Pulitzer Prize several years ago. He had few of the instincts of a journalist, and he scarcely ever left the confines of his town house in Georgetown to seek firsthand information; rather, the information came to him in the persons of high government officials who came to lunch graciously with him and to proffer their versions of the inside poop.

I always scanned his columns for possible errors of fact, and when I had time, fiddled with his prose, breaking long sentences into short ones and switching cases from passive to active. He liked what I did, and thought I was a superb editor. It was through him that Costigan got my name when he was returning to New York with the first draft of his book. I'm not sure old Otto did me a favor.

Today, I put his column into the works pretty much as written. Dull, but no errors. I continued to go through the motions of processing columns and comic strips, feeling slightly removed from reality. On most days of the week, I performed my chores in solitude, but Wednesdays had somehow evolved into visitation days. Ben Kamen, the humor columnist, came in and told me some jokes that weren't very funny. He was a terrible joke teller, yet his columns were very funny—that is, until you discerned his formula, which was the switcheroo of shoe-on-the-other-foot gimmick. For instance, regarding parents who were concerned about drug use by their children, he wrote as if the parents were the users and the children were exhorting them to go straight. Very funny and occasionally the vehicle of valuable insights, but more often tedious and predictable.

Godbold came to the door and told me there would be seventy-five guests at the Tavern party for Cosgrove. He had Rocky Caputo, the puzzle editor, with him, and I was burdened with two weeks of crossword puzzles.

At eleven, I called Tom Costigan, not because I really wanted to talk to him but because I remembered that I had forgotten to give him Danny Dunn's message.

He said snottily, "I'm amazed that you remembered."

I said, "How's Alice's kitchen coming?"

He emitted some expletives. "The damned insurance company claims we're not covered. They say that damage by hand grenade is an act of war, and acts of war are excluded from their coverage."

"You're not going to stand for that," I said.

"Hell, no," he said. "They'll pay; you better believe it."

Knowing Costigan, I was sure that they would. "Meanwhile, Alice will be without a kitchen."

He said he got the name of a contractor from Joey Gargano and was going ahead with the repairs.

"Gargano!" I exclaimed.

"Why not," Costigan said. "He owes me one. Besides, it'll give me a chance to see how the system works."

What I saw was a slight chink in his integrity—he wouldn't deal with Gargano to save Times Square, but he would when it was a question of saving himself a substantial amount of money.

The cartoonists arrived at noon. They came on like creatures from *National Lampoon's Animal House.* I always had the impression that I heard circus music heralding the clowns, and that they were crawling all over me like frisky lizards. There were just five of them today, creating the commotion of fifty.

Cartooning is a lonely profession pursued by perennial adolescents. They sit alone in their homes or studios before tilted tables, staring at white oblongs of cardboard, and pray to St. Rube Goldberg for inspiration. They get lonelier than the Maytag repair man. So when they get released, they're like children bursting out at recess. I generally enjoy their company; over the years, those who were in the New York vicinity had built a tradition of lunching with me on Wednesdays in a nearby hamburger-and-beer joint. About once a month, I would pick up the tab—over Godbold's howls of protest. Today I wasn't in the mood to lunch in pandemonium, but I couldn't break the tradition.

I had once made the mistake of telling them of my stretch in the seminary, and it was Mort Laser who started calling me "Father" Carey and referring to himself and the other cartoonists as "Father Carey's chickens." And naturally, I had to say grace before lunch, a somewhat scatological version of Grandpa Sycamore's in *You Can't Take It With You.* Mort, from Brooklyn, did a hillbilly strip called "Hey, Rube!" Dick Shine, who was in his late fifties, did a teenage strip. Bud Hicks, originally from Kentucky, did a sophisticated Yuppie strip. And Helen Hills, a magnificently homely young woman, was the creator of "Pamela," featuring a gorgeous sexpot fighting off the advances of a hundred million randy males, one at a time.

The fifth cartoonist today was young David Glass, the different one. He tried to fit in with the others, but he had no talent for impromptu banter or ready laughter. His attempts at verbal wit were painful, and yet his comic strip, "Mayor Baldi," was both clever and funny. Baldi was a short, rotund version of New York's Mayor Koch, and his Seaport City was a simplified microcosm of all cities and, indeed, nations.

I flipped through the strips, intending to go over them more thoroughly after lunch. The ones by Glass struck me as odd, but I didn't have time to study them. I said, "Come back with me after lunch, okay?"

Glass nodded.

It was always hard to get out to lunch without being stopped en route at least twice. Godbold flagged me into his office. "No free lunches today, understand?" he said.

I said, "Yes, sir, boss, sir."

The other interrupter was Max Abel, the personal-finance columnist. I told the cartoonists to stampede on ahead to the restaurant, and that I would join them there in a few minutes. Then I waved Max into my office. He protested, saying he didn't want to hold me back from my lunch date.

I said, "Frankly, I'd rather chew the fat with you, Max. I'm in no mood for loud noises and practical jokes today."

"Just for a minute, Eddie," he said. He sighed like a tired old man as he lowered his body into a chair. That was not like the Max Abel I knew, the sixty-year-old satyr who looked eighty-five and acted eighteen. He was a slender little guy with close-cropped, curly brown hair turning gray and a ruddy face with tightly rumpled skin. Today his face was ashen.

When I expressed my concern, he growled that he was fit as a fiddle. He was one of those unprepossessing men who, nevertheless, seemed to be attractive to gorgeous women of all ages; he had supreme confidence in his sexual prowess and an unfeigned desire to please as many women as he could in his lifetime. He didn't understand my monkish lifestyle, and he was often trying to "fix me up" with one or another of his ravishing beauties. Not today. He mumbled something about "the old prostate" acting up—which, Lord knows, it had every right to do—but I had the impression that his ailment was more psychological than physical. He seemed troubled.

I liked and admired the old buzzard, and wished I could help. I told him that we had just added the *Honolulu Star-Bulletin* to his list, and he said, "Aloha." The news didn't thrill him. Actually, he was well off financially and didn't need the money. He held a high position in the hierarchy of the mighty Mid-Manhattan Bank, and he wrote the column for us as a sideline. I think his motive in writing it was an altruistic desire to help the thousands of less fortunate readers who were letting their money dribble away. In my opinion, it was the best personal-finance column in the business.

He sighed again when he stood up. I sensed that he had come to tell me something and had decided not to.

I said, "I have all the time in the world."

"No, you run along," he said. "Go play with the children."

The lunch went as expected. Bud Hicks spilled soup in his lap and complained to the waiter, "Waiter, there's soup in my fly." The waiter groaned. Mort Laser wanted to know why they were called waiters. "We're the waiters," he said. "They should be called 'servers' or 'plate-bearers to the gods.'" Other appellations were suggested, and everyone had a good time, including me.

David Glass came back to the office with me and sat in uneasy silence while I studied the two weeks of strips. He was a good-looking, almost pretty young man with the trim figure of an Olympic runner. I once grabbed his upper arm for some reason, probably to guide him in some direction, and discovered hard muscle there. It was obvious that he exercised regularly. But when I asked him about it, he looked away in embarrassment. I sympathized with him, figuring he had as many hangups as I had. Busty Helen Hills tried to catch his interest early on, but Dave just looked puzzled. He wasn't simply a misogynist but an all-encompassing misanthrope. Or at least that was my reading of him.

I came to the cartoon sequence that had bothered me. Mayor Baldi of Seaport City is feuding with a twin city, called Portsea City, which Baldi believes should be incorporated into his. Baldi finds a Portsea spy in his headquarters, and he magnanimously lets him go. Then, giggling, he drops a bomb on the spy from a second-floor window of City Hall. "Ker-boom!" Limbs go flying. Baldi says, "Ha! Now he doesn't have a leg to stand on!"

I raised my eyes to Glass. He was looking at my shoulder the way Father Garvin did. I said, "I don't get it, Dave."

"Oh, come on, Father!" he said. "It's a visual pun. It takes an old expression and illustrates it literally. Don't you see, he's blown apart, so he doesn't have a leg to stand on. His legs are gone."

I rubbed my face. Cartoonists are sensitive souls when

it comes to their brainchildren, and they can be terribly wounded if you tell them their idea isn't funny. "I get it, Dave," I said slowly. "I think it's damn clever, and if I showed this to the other cartoonists, they'd fall all over themselves laughing. I know that. But it's black humor, and that's something you have to be careful of with the general public. Some readers will love it and others will be offended."

"Offended?" he said. "How can they be, when something's as funny as this is? You yourself admit it's funny, don't you?"

I began to doubt my own reaction to the strip. On another day, I might have thought it funny. Today, I didn't. "We-ell," I said. "I'm just trying to put myself in the place of the reader."

"Father," he said, "the strip is funny. Take my word for it."

I saw that if I rejected the strip, I'd have a fearfully unhappy cartoonist on my hands. Besides, not many readers were likely to come upon the strip the day after being themselves the targets of a murderous bombing designed to leave them without a leg to stand on. I relented and let the strip go through unchanged. Glass departed, undoubtedly feeling that he had triumphed over a blue-nosed philistine.

I ran out of gas soon after that. I told Godbold I was going to the Tom Jones Tavern to check on preparations for the party. But I lied. I headed crosstown toward home, making a detour to the Costigan house, where I found Alice bemusedly watching a plumber and assistant messing around in the kitchen. The debris was gone.

I said, "He's a fast worker."

She said, "Who?"

"Joey Gargano."

She said, "Strange, isn't it?"

She turned down my invitation to dine with me at Vinnie's. "I think I better stick with Da," she said. "And afterward, I have some papers to correct."

I looked down, and, sure enough, the bulky briefcase

was in her left hand. It seemed to be a living part of her arm.

We embraced perfunctorily, and I went down the stairs. Fortunately, I didn't bump into Costigan. I was bruised enough for one day.

I dragged myself home, made myself a very large, very dry martini, heated something from the freezer, and ate mechanically in front of the TV set. ABC News showed the nineteen dead bodies in Beirut and the five dead bodies in Canarsie. Hurricane Colleen was shying away from the Florida coast and spinning toward Hatteras, but a high from the Midwest was likely to keep the rude storm from barging into the Middle Atlantic States. I occasionally talk back to the set. I said to the forecaster, "Knowing that, I'll sleep better tonight."

My head was ready for sleep, but the rest of me wasn't. I walk a lot. I like walking; it's my only exercise. I went out, and walked. The sky was now clear. The high must have arrived. I said, "Hi." I occasionally talk to the sky. I walked for several hours. I wound up at Philbin's Irish Pub. No reason, just that it was there.

Most of the faces were familiar, but there was nobody I wanted to talk to. I had a beer and went home.

I was ready for sleep. I went through the nightly rituals and got into bed. It would be fun to have a pet to come home to, I thought. I remembered the Irish setter I'd had as a boy in Brooklyn. Mike. That was a dog who knew how to greet a person. He knocked you down and licked your face. "Hi, Mike," I said into the darkness.

Just as sleep was descending, I thought of David Glass's comic strip. I groaned. Of all the miserable things to think of! I saw the Portsea spy being blown apart by Mayor Baldi's bomb. I saw the spy's face as Glass had drawn it, and I knew why the strip had made me feel so uncomfortable. It wasn't the cartoonist's apparent advocacy of "Bomb Thy Neighbor." All slapstick was cruel. No, what made me squirm in bed was the face of the spy. It was the bulldog face of Tom Costigan.

4

The second attempt on Tom Costigan's life was a resounding success, and, God help me, I saw it happen. The only way the police could have prevented it would have been to take him into custody and put him in solitary.

Let's see, the second day after the skylight bombing was Thursday, and the Cosgrove party was slated for Friday. On Thursday, nothing much happened. By then, my nervous system was over the screaming meemies, and I got through the day with equanimity if not my usual bounding spirits.

Lieutenant Ferrante visited me at the office, primarily to get the originals of every "Stranglehold" column that Costigan had ever written for us, not the edited versions that had appeared in the paper. He was interested in the potentially libelous material I had cut out.

While we waited for the dog-eared manuscripts to be dug out of the files, he said, "How long have you known Costigan?"

I told him three years.

"Do you have any suggestions?"

My poor undernourished brain had been picking at the attempted murder for two days, and all it had come up with was the dumb quotation from a grade-school memory book: "I thought and thought and thought in vain/Until I thought I'd sign my name. Yours truly, Edward Carey."

I said, "I think you're on the right track, Lieutenant, that's all I can say. Costigan is an abrasive man, and he's made a lot of people hate him. But at the same time, he's an honorable man. He hasn't cheated anybody, and he hasn't seduced anybody's wife. So while people hate him, they don't hate him enough to try to kill him.

"Therefore, the answer probably lies in the enemies he's made through his column. But that doesn't help you much, does it? He has taken on nearly every corrupt group in the country, not only organized crime. He's been particularly tough on some giant corporations who corrupt congressmen more subtly than with packets of cash. You'll see when you study the columns.

"And he has files on corrupters he hasn't even mentioned yet. As you know, he gets his information from a network of snitches across the country. And he protects those sources. That's why he hasn't been completely open with you. Not that he thinks you're corrupt, but there are corrupt policemen on every force in the country. So it's possible that the answer doesn't lie in these past columns, but in a column he hasn't written yet."

"Like what?"

"God, I don't know, Lieutenant," I said. "The other night, he mentioned an upcoming column that was going to be a shocker."

Ferrante held up next week's column, which I had given him. "This one?"

"I doubt it. That's about the carting industry in the New York area with special focus on Joey Gargano. It may hurt Gargano's business, but it's not going to put him in jail. Besides, you've already checked him out.

Frankly, Tom Costigan was drinking at the time, and it's possible he said that just to get a rise out of us. That's one of his faults. He brags."

In response to my question, Ferrante told me what the police had come up with, and it added up to zilch. "Dozens of people had access to the roofs at that time," he said. "We went over the list with Costigan, but he wasn't much help. He'd say, 'Yeah, yeah, I know him,' or 'That wimp? You're kidding!' It's almost as if he *wants* the killer to have another go at him.... Does he strike you as potentially suicidal?"

"Good Lord, no," I said. "On the contrary, having survived two attempts at murder, he probably regards himself as indestructible. It's part of his arrogance."

"*Two* attempts, you say?"

I told him about the bullet through the window down in Virginia, and my theory that it was meant to intimidate rather than kill.

Ferrante agreed. "When the Mafia wants to kill, they generally succeed," he said.

That night, Alice and I watched the sunset from the roof of my apartment building. Being fans of old movies, I was Cary Grant and she was Katharine Hepburn, a role she fit better than I fit mine. But what the hell, everyone wants to be debonair once in a while.

When the last of my neighbors retreated to their apartments and we were alone in the soft darkness, we got ourselves in a fierce embrace that we seemed unable to break. Finally, we both said, "Phew!" Cary and Kate never said "Phew" in their lives.

I invited her to come down to my apartment so that we could take up the matter where we had left off, but naturally I couched it as a joke, and naturally she declined.

She said, "Do you give out rain checks?"

I said, "No, it's now or never."

She touched my cheek with the tips of her fingers. She said, "Another time, dear. We'll have something to look forward to, won't we?"

It took me a long time to get to sleep that night.

The entrance to the Tom Jones Tavern was off Central Park South, not far from the Plaza Hotel. The front facade and the cozy waiting room immediately inside the entrance were the only attempts at replication of an old-English countryside inn. The rest of the rambling structure was mostly glass and glittering crystal, which gave the illusion of outdoor dining with a view of trees on either side and of the pond in the rear. When it first opened back in the Thirties, the operators established a colony of swans in the pond as part of the decor; but successive swan families quickly disappeared—I'm told that roast swan is tougher than turkey, but who cared during the Depression?—and they gave up the attempt.

It was one of the costliest places in the city to throw a bash, but it reeked of class, and both Horace Hawthorne and Chuck Godbold—the same Godbold who frowned on my picking up tabs at hamburger-and-beer joints—liked the reek, and justified the expense by saying that nothing was too good for such a great cultural hero as J. P. Cosgrove. Our party was in the west area, partitioned from the rest of the restaurant by opaque glass panels.

The engraved invitations read: "Cocktails at seven, buffet dinner at eight." Since our guests included cartoonists, this arrangement was a mistake. Among my chores for the evening were staying close and keeping them from rampaging. The males came dressed in jackets and ties for a change, the female in an honest-to-God party dress, and they acted almost civilized for all of ten minutes.

Then Mort Laser pasted on a black mustache and went into his Groucho Marx act. Bud Hicks told hillbilly stories that included loud barnyard imitations, Dick

Shine became all Three Stooges simultaneously, and Helen Hills, after only one drink, told anyone who came near her to "stop pawing me." A trio of musicians played sedate music, and I got someone to dance with Helen until her feeling of sexual embattlement passed. David Glass sat on a barstool, watching and trying to react, but he was always one tick behind, so that he appeared on the verge of saying something and then not saying it.

When Tom Costigan arrived, I peered at him closely for signs of trouble. There weren't any. He appeared to be in a passive good humor. He brought Alice as his date for the evening. Clothed in an elegant, pale-blue cocktail gown and given her unselfconsciously dignified bearing, she was royalty among dressed-up peasants. And when father and daughter danced together, she gracefully followed his vintage Lindy, deep swoops and all.

Then Costigan headed for the bar.

I intercepted him, fearing that a Costigan fired with booze could be a bigger headache than all of the cartoonists put together. I introduced him to David Glass.

"But you two must know each other," I said. "Where did you meet?"

Costigan looked at Glass in puzzlement. "Did we meet, David?"

Glass said, "Not that I remember, sir. I recognize you from your picture in the paper, that's all."

Costigan scowled at me. "What made you think we had met?" he asked.

"I don't know," I said, kicking myself. "Just that David drew a character that looked like you, and so I thought maybe—"

Costigan swung his attention back to Glass. "What do you draw, David?"

Glass lowered his eyes in modesty. "A comic strip. Called 'Mayor Baldi.'"

"Oh, yes," Costigan said. "Oh, yes." Then he said, "It's not very funny, is it?"

I took his arm and said, "I want you to meet some of the other cartoonists." And I made some stumbling introductions, away from a red-faced David Glass, who was staring down into his drink.

Costigan said expansively, "What's happened to the funny sheets, fellers? They're not half as good as they used to be. The last good strip was 'Popeye.' Why aren't there any more 'Popeyes'?"

Mort Laser waggled an imaginary cigar and said, "Because the mental age of the reader has gone up. How old are you, Mr. Costigan?"

Bud Hicks said, "Are you an ex-wrestler, Mr. Costigan? Don't you write that whatchamacallit, 'Stranglehold'?"

Dick Shine said, "Cut it out, guys. Don't you recognize Wimpy? How about a hamburger, sir?"

Helen Hills batted her eyes up at Costigan. "I can tell you're a gentleman of the old school, Mr. Costigan. I just adore gentlemen of the old school. Is that the old school tie you're wearing?"

Costigan glared at me.

I said, "Sorry, Tom, they belong to the Don Rickles school of comedy. What they're saying is they're happy to meet you."

Costigan said, "What do you have to do to get a drink around here?"

I let him go. There was just so much one man could do to avert disaster.

Alice was at my elbow. She had been there through the whole exchange. I started to introduce her, but she interrupted by saying sweetly, "I'm Wimpy's daughter." To Helen Hills she said, "Are you Olive Oyl?"

That fractured the cartoonists. They called their stout female buddy "Olive" for the rest of the night.

The party was getting crowded, and the overall hum of voices was rising. I was on duty, circulating, introducing, laughing, telling jokes, replenishing drinks. I didn't mind.

44

I liked seventy-three of the seventy-five people who were there. Besides, I had fortified myself at the beginning with a very large, bone-dry martini.

I didn't have to worry about guest of honor J. P. Cosgrove, a hulking wreck of a man in a heavy tweed suit, for my two bosses, Godbold and Hawthorne, were dancing around him like worshipful acolytes. At one point, a scent reminiscent of my altar-boy days reached me, and for a moment I thought they were sanctifying him with incense, but it was only Otto Walters's dipso wife, who must have splashed too much cologne on her ample body. Horace Hawthorne wanted Godbold and me to set up a reception line, so people could file by and pay obeisance to their literary god; but we talked him into a stately march around the room instead, and then a retreat to the table on the dais. J. P. moved through the throng like an arthritic pope of Rome dispensing blessings.

He didn't sweat. Despite his ridiculous winter garb on a warm September evening, Cosgrove's puffy face was as dry as bleached bones in a desert. Once enthroned on the dais, he sipped Perrier water and acted deaf, dumb, blind, and asleep. In fairness to the man, I must report that he had had more than his share of serious illnesses in recent years, including two heart attacks and the loss of half a stomach to ulcers. Despite his martyred air, his calorie intake was apparently still sufficient to maintain his elephantine physique.

Max Abel, the personal-finance columnist, provided the biggest surprise. He arrived proudly escorting his date for the evening, Honor O'Toole. He looked like Pappy Yokum with Daisy Mae. The cartoonists went gaga over such blatant pulchritude. Groucho slunk and rolled his eyes. Bud Hicks crowed and flapped his arms. The Three Stooges acted like the Three Stooges.

Tom Costigan was the first to reach her, however. He whirled her off to waltz, though the music was 1940s swing.

Max followed her with his eyes.

I said, "You amaze me, old man. That's more broad than you can handle."

He focused on me. "Oh, hi, Eddie. Ain't she something?"

"She's the toast of Hell's Kitchen," I said. "How did you get to meet her?"

His eyes slid away from me. "It's a long story," he said. I saw that he wasn't going to tell me the long story.

I shook my head in wonder. "I've lusted in my heart for that magnificent piece of art," I said. "And here you have her gift-wrapped and holding a bill of sale."

"Piece of art?" he said. "Eddie, you don't know a piece of art from a piece of tail."

"Sometimes they're the same thing," I said, slightly wounded by the put-down. "When that happens, I imagine the price tag is astronomical."

He lowered his eyes. "Eddie, if you only knew," he said.

Dick Shine was dancing with her now. He was a very short man, and his nose was in her décolletage. His reactions of exaggerated awe were really very funny, and most of the observers were laughing. Max Abel wasn't laughing.

While performing my troubleshooting chores, I did manage to get in half a dance with Alice.

"I see Miss Cleavage is here," she said.

"I hadn't noticed."

"That's Da's second drink."

"Wouldn't it be wonderful if he and J. P. had a fight?"

"They couldn't."

"Why not?"

"Cosgrove hasn't moved in ten minutes. I think he's dead."

"No such luck. He's posing for a statue."

Max Abel cut in, and I resumed circulating. The cartoonists and Costigan seemed to be behaving themselves. I strolled past the partition into the main dining area to take a two-minute breather. Despite its cool and airy look, the place was jam-packed with fat wallets and sleek women.

Two of the dining parties gave me a start. While I vaguely realized that politicians and underworld figures came here seeking dress-up respectability, it struck me as odd that both Joey Gargano and Hugh Mullen chose this particular night to dine in class at the crystal palace. Gargano sat with three spiffily dressed gentlemen, all in dark-blue suits, at a table against the glass wall under a small red sign that said EXIT. The table blocked the exit. Not much animation there. Cool.

Mullen's table-for-two was on the opposite side of the room. His companion was the Hibernian Rod McKuen, Brendan Power. Since both the politician and the poet were addicted to the sound of their own voices, it was obvious that a nonstop conversation was going on.

I had no desire to gab with either group. My only concern was to keep Tom Costigan from discovering Gargano's presence and working himself up into a bullish mood amid all that glass.

I stepped back, and stepped on Costigan's toe. "Oops, sorry," I said.

"That's okay, Eddie," he said. The mildness of his tone frightened me.

I took his arm and said, "Let's go back."

"In a minute," he said. "I have to say hello to Joey."

Reluctantly, I followed him to Gargano's table. They greeted each other in what seemed like cordial tones.

Gargano said, "You know the boys."

I didn't know the boys, and I was pretty sure that Costigan didn't, either. The boys showed no emotion in their faces.

"How's my man doing?" Gargano asked.

"Pretty good, Joey. The place looks better than it did before somebody blew it up."

"Good, good."

Costigan actually had a half-smile on his face. He said, "That damn explosion made me think of the time we blew old man Keenan's ashcan apart. Remember? What was it, a five-incher?"

Gargano nodded. "They don't sell them anymore. It's a shame."

"I guess too many kids blew themselves up. Was that the first time you were nabbed by the cops?"

"Come on, Tom, we weren't arrested," Gargano protested mildly.

"No, just detained, but it felt like being arrested. We had some good times, though, didn't we?"

"Yeah, we did."

I was amazed. They were reminiscing about their boyhood.

Costigan said, "That was no five-incher that came through the skylight."

"I guess not."

"Stick to five-inchers, Joey."

"You do the same."

"See you around."

"Yeah. Let me know you need anything."

"Right."

As we threaded our way back toward the Cosgrove party, Costigan noticed Hugh Mullen and Brendan Power waving to him. He waved back, then said to me in a low voice, "Look at them smile. The Irish canary doesn't know that his tootsie is in there rubbing bellies with that banker friend of yours. I think I'll go tell him."

I grabbed him and held him back.

He grinned at me. "Okay, Eddie. The dumb bastard probably wouldn't slug Abel, anyway. He'd recite a poem at him."

Having gotten Costigan back to our own party with no bones broken, I felt I had earned another drink. People were lining up at the buffet table, but the bar was still open. I made my own martini, then strolled toward the buffet table, where a little flurry of activity was taking place. The cartoonists were having a Swedish-meatball fight, using spoons as slingshots. I rushed to break it up, and a meatball bounced off my chest and landed in my drink.

I had to clown a bit to quiet them, acting as if the meatball were an olive, spearing it with a toothpick and nibbling. I said they had created a new drink, "a cartooni."

I sat with the cartoonists. Costigan and Alice sat on the dais with the big shots. Costigan smiled a lot, but his voice was loud. From the fragments I heard, I believe he managed to insult everyone there, despite the shushing whispers of Alice.

To Otto Walters: "I love your column, Otto. I just wish I could read it without falling asleep. To me—"

"Shush, Da."

"To me, it's Nyquil."

He had similar compliments for some of the others, but the choicest he reserved for the guest of honor. "I'm a horror-story nut, J. P., but your books were the biggest horrors of them all."

And again: "Out of curiosity, how could you bring yourself to write about those people, those bloated English-American plutocrats, you being Irish and all that, and then turn around and imitate them, for God's sake? Your lace curtain is showing, old man."

I glanced at the object of his attention. Old J. P. Cosgrove was still posing for a statue.

And so the festive occasion went. Horace Hawthorne made a speech, then J. P. got up, mumbled about twenty words, and sat down again. Hawthorne invited the reporters present to ask questions. One woman said, "Do you consider yourself washed-up?" and that was the end of that.

After the meal, the guests moved about, some to the bar, some to the rest rooms, some outside for a breath of air. I heard someone order a stinger, and suddenly I needed one very badly. My chores for the evening were about over, and I was entitled to relax.

I saw David Glass talking to Alice. He had her hand

in his, and it seemed to me she was gently trying to pull hers away.

She saw me approaching and said, "Get Da."

"Where is he?"

"He said he needed some air."

"Right."

I placed my stinger on a ledge where I hoped it wouldn't be disturbed, and went looking for Costigan. There was no exit to the outdoors from our party area, so I went out into the general restaurant area. Joey Gargano was still at his table, but seemed to have lost one of his boys, whom I idly assumed had gone to the gents' room. The table at which Hugh Mullen and Brendan Power had sat was vacant.

I strolled outdoors into the cool semidarkness. Spills of light from the restaurant illuminated the nearby lawn, making the far reaches and the trees bordering it all the darker. Near the front of the building, where the wall was solid, the blackness was almost complete. There was a moist softness in the air that was most pleasant. I stretched and peered around while my eyes adjusted to the darkness.

There was no one on the illuminated portion of the lawn. Farther out, about a hundred feet from where I was standing, were the tree trunks. One of them moved, and I saw that it was a man, his face raised to the sky. Tom Costigan. I watched in fascination, since I seldom saw him in repose, and wondered if he was simply reading the signs of tomorrow's weather or praying to God for forgiveness for all the little hurts he had inflicted. I smiled to myself at the latter thought, knowing that he was totally unaware of any lack of charity in himself.

Something flew through the air in a high arc from the blackness to my left. I hadn't seen anything or heard anything before my peripheral vision picked up the hurtling object. It landed in the soft grass at Costigan's feet. In the one second he had, he stepped back a step, raised his hand in a warding-off gesture, and I heard him say one word: "Christ!"

Then the explosion tore him apart, and I was sitting down, clutching a pain in my shoulder.

The sound reverberated in my skull, and I heard nothing else. I saw Costigan fall, and saw nothing else. My hand was sticky with my own blood, and all I could think—if Tom Costigan knew, he would have nodded and said it was typical—all I could think was, Damn it, there goes my only good suit.

5

I sat on the grass while my brain staggered about trying to sort things out. It came up with overlapping messages. Costigan is dead. Nothing I can do about that. No need to move. Peripheral vision: Three dark-clad figures move quickly from side door to parking lot, one shaped like a giant salami. Gargano and friends. Dumb move. Police will know they were here. A prayer: Dear God, have mercy on Costigan. You're right, I dreamed of murdering him, I admit it, but what I really felt was, when you come right down to it—nuts, I'm probably lying to myself again—no, what I really felt was, If belittling me made him feel good, well, why not let him, because he had shown me time and again that he actually respected me, and— I don't know what I mean. I refuse to feel guilty, however, because I sure'n hell didn't throw that grenade.

I heard rustlings behind me, gasps, murmurs, people emerging from the restaurant to see what the explosion was about. My stomach was acting up. I still clutched my left shoulder with the vague idea of holding it together.

A voice quite close to me said, "Jesus, Mary, and

Joseph!" I recognized the voice of Hugh Mullen, and I pictured him blessing himself, the pious fraud.

Another voice said, "Alas, poor Costigan, I knew him well." Supercilious. I wanted to jump up and smash the snotty poet in the face, but I was concentrating on keeping my dinner down. There was more saliva in my mouth than I knew what to do with.

So Mullen and Brendan Power were still here, I thought. Their table had been empty, but they hadn't departed. They were standing near me, over a hundred feet from the bloody corpse, and yet they knew that the corpse was Costigan's. How could that be? The freshets of saliva were subsiding. I thought of vomiting on their shoes, but I couldn't decide which shoes were theirs.

Alice. The thought of her brought me to my feet. More than twenty people were standing in clusters behind me, Alice striding through them, her eyes fixed on the crumpled figure at the far end of the lawn. I called her name sharply and moved to intercept her.

She glared at me. "It's him, isn't it?" she said.

I started to explain that I had come out but was too late to prevent—

She brushed past me and continued toward her father's body.

I lurched after her, saying, "No" and "Don't."

Her words came back to me. "I've got to see him."

And then she stood there, gazing downward.

I saw what she saw, him on his back, his torso looking like something in a butcher shop, a leg at a crazy angle beside him, his face comparatively untouched, with only one deep gash across his cheek. His eyes were open.

She said, "Eddie, close his eyes."

I closed them with my left hand.

She leaned over and made the Sign of the Cross on his forehead. Then, moving back a step, she lowered herself slowly to her knees, her hands in the prayerful position of children and of sisters in a convent, and she prayed.

Soundlessly. I flopped to my knees beside her, sat back on my heels, and tried to think of a prayer to say. This is insane; God save Alice. This is insane; God save Alice.

A policeman led us away from the scene and into the manager's office in the restaurant. Before we entered the structure, I saw the cartoonists standing in the darkness near the building. Mort Laser called, "Are you okay, Father?" I gave him a slight wave. David Glass stood there, not part of the group, seemingly in shock. I wondered if he was awed at his prophetic cartoon coming true: Costigan no longer with a leg to stand on.

Alice sat in a straight-back chair, her body rigid, her face dreadfully composed. I told her I was sorry, and she said, "It wasn't your fault, Eddie. You couldn't have stopped it."

I said, "It's true, damn it." Then I said, "He was a martyr, you know. He had a holy mission—"

"It wasn't holy, Eddie," she said. "He just liked to fight."

The next hour was a jumble in my mind. I was oppressed by bulky men in blue uniforms. I told my story at least four times to a succession of putty faces. They were very patient with me. "That's all I know," I said. "I'm pretty sure that the one who threw the bomb was standing in the shadow of the building near the front. That's where you should be looking."

"Looking for what?"

"I don't know. Clues! Footprints, cigarette butts, whatever detectives look for."

"It won't show anything, Mr. Carey. It's been trampled by a mess of people from the restaurant. Besides, we don't think the killer was standing there."

"Where do you think he was standing?"

"Where you were standing, Mr. Carey."

I thought that was the funniest thing I had heard all night. I laughed until Alice said, "Stop it, Eddie. They're saying you did it."

In the face of this insanity, I tried a rational approach.

"Look at my shoulder, for God's sake! Do you really think I would stand there in open ground and take a chance on blowing myself up? That'd be suicidal, for crying out loud!"

The putty face said, "You wouldn't be the first one it's happened to. What we don't get is where you hid the grenade."

I had difficulty concentrating on the policemen's words. "Hid the grenade?" I repeated dumbly.

"You obviously didn't carry it in your pocket all night. Where was it?"

I said, "The only thing I hid was a stinger, and I could sure use it right now."

"Is that what you call it, a stinger?"

I couldn't see the policeman's face very clearly, and my mind fumbled for words.

"Officer!" Alice said sharply. "Over here, Officer!" The blurry face, which had been close to mine, receded.

"You are making an absurd ass of yourself," she said. "Mr. Carey is my fiancé, and he is bleeding. He doesn't need your imbecilic bullying, he needs medical attention. And he needs it *now*."

I marveled at the tone of command in her voice and at the promptness with which an ambulance attendant appeared to fuss with my wound. But most of all, I marveled at her statement that I was her "fiancé." I thought about that. I felt both elated and frightened. She deserved better than a neurotic person like me. Then I figured she had used the word just to shut the dumb cop up and that she really didn't mean it literally.

Lieutenant Fred Ferrante arrived and put a final halt to the badgering by the cops. "Mr. Carey doesn't make enemies," he told them. My boss, Chuck Godbold, said the same thing. My thank-you's came out like snarls. I was turning surly, and the fact that the bloody wound in my shoulder required only two stitches, a dash of sulfa powder, and a Band-Aid didn't improve my disposition. A *Band-Aid!* I had cast myself in a semiheroic role in my mind. Now I wasn't even that: two stitches do not a hero make. The Band-Aid, even though a large one, made me a buffoon.

Brendan Power, full of good cheer, somehow charmed himself into the room. "I hear the police thought you did it," he said. "Hoist with your own petard, as it were. I'm glad that's not so, Eddie, but it would have been interesting, wouldn't it?"

I said, "Thank you for comforting me, Brendan."

Abruptly, he was cloaked in solemnity as he turned to Alice. He expressed his deep poetic sorrow, and said, "Hugh Mullen asks if he can be of help. As you know, he runs a funeral establishment. He can take a multitude of unpleasant burdens off your shoulder."

For the first time, Alice was close to tears. "That would be . . . very helpful," she said. "One other thing—a priest."

"Father Garvin is with him now," Power said softly, theatrically.

At length, Lieutenant Ferrante said that we were free to leave, and offered to have a squad car drive us home.

Alice's face took on a stricken look. "The checkroom stub, Eddie," she said.

"What about it?"

"It was in Da's pocket."

"I'm sure we don't need the stub," I said. "What was it? A coat?"

"My briefcase."

"Oh, for crying out loud."

We retrieved the briefcase, and a police car took us back to Hell's Kitchen. I got out with her at the Costigan house. It was utterly dark; not even a hall light had been left on. It looked like what it was—a house of death.

I put my good arm around her shoulder and felt her shudder. "Are you sure you want to go in?" I asked.

She straightened. "Certainly," she said, and marched up the outside steps to the front door.

I followed her. "I need a drink," I said.

She turned to look down at me with half a smile on her face. "You're *all* Irish, Eddie, despite what you say." She touched my cheek with her fingertips. "Come on up."

We sat on the ripped sofa side by side. Since her new kitchen was not yet functioning, I fetched the necessaries from her father's liquor closet and made stiff drinks for the two of us, an appropriate beginning for an Irish wake.

I touched her shoulder. It was rigid. "You're holding your breath," I said.

She exhaled and slumped against me. "He was a good man, Eddie," she said.

"That he was," I said fervently, like a full-blooded Irishman.

She shook her head in misery. "God takes the good ones and lets the evil ones live on," she said. "There's something wrong with that."

I wanted to say that God had nothing to do with it, but that would have opened a theological can of worms, which I wasn't ready to face, so I said nothing.

"I'll have to redo this sofa," she said. "What pattern should I make it?"

"Black and tan," I said, for no good reason at all.

"No," she said. "It would keep reminding me of my father. Do you think St. Vincent de Paul will take it like this?"

"I'm sure they will."

She stirred. "Your poor suit. Let me soak it."

I said, "The jacket's not worth saving. Don't worry about it."

After a while, she said, "Who did it, Eddie?"

I sighed. "The obvious one seems to be Joey Gargano. He was there, you know."

"So the policeman said."

"He didn't do it himself, I can testify to that. He came out of the restaurant right after the explosion. The one who did it was already outside. It's possible it was one of

Gargano's thugs. I saw that one was gone when I went out to look for Tom. But I don't think so. It doesn't make sense."

"Why?"

"It just seems to me that if Gargano wanted your father dead, he sure wouldn't show up at the scene himself. That'd be dumb. Hell, he'd be at his usual table at Vinnie's surrounded by a dozen alibi witnesses. Him being at the tavern doesn't make sense. Besides, from seeing the two of them together, I'd swear that he and Tom still liked each other, no matter what."

"But Da was gunning for him. Those columns had to hurt."

"He was gunning for a lot of people, honey, and it's obvious that one of them—not Gargano—didn't want to fight according to Tom's rules."

"A sneaking, cowardly killer."

"That's all there are these days," I said. "No more shootouts at the O.K. Corral or showdowns at high noon, just bushwhackers striking from ambush. And if you think about it, it makes more sense to the—"

"The devil with sense!"

I said, "Right."

My arm was around her, her thigh was warm against mine, and we were alone, but each of us was drooping with shock, grief, and fatigue. Surely it wasn't a time for sexual play, and yet a part of me was becoming alarmingly aroused—an instinctive resurgence of life after a brush with death, I had read somewhere.

I shifted positions and said, "I need another drink."

Then I saw that she was crying, and I did my best to soothe her.

Before I left, I went down to Tom's bedroom and picked out what looked like his best blue suit, a shirt, tie, socks, and shoes to take to Mullen's Funeral Parlor in the morning for his wake.

When I got to my apartment, I dumped the clothes on the sofa and dragged myself to the bedroom. Nuts to everything else; I was pooped. So naturally the doorbell rang. I peered at the bedside clock: 12:55. No fit time for man or beast to be prowling in apartment hallways. I sat on the side of the bed and waited for whatever it was to go away. It didn't. It rang again.

I shuffled through the living room in my stocking feet and put my eye to the peephole in the door. "Shit," I muttered, and opened the door.

Father Frank Garvin said, "Is it all right, Eddie?"

If I interpreted the look in his glassy eyes correctly, he was pleading to come in on a matter of desperate urgency. It was the look of a bedeviled man.

I stood back to let him glide by. He pirouetted in the middle of my living room and faced me.

"Are you sure it's all right?"

"Sure, tomorrow's Saturday," I told him. "Sit down."

He paced, pranced for a moment like a high-strung dog, and perched on the sofa. He said, "The church needs you, Eddie. You don't go to Mass anymore."

"Maybe once in a while," I said. "I'll try to go more often."

"Good," he said, and stared at me mutely.

I decided not to offer him a drink. It was obvious that he already had a snootful.

He said, "I gave the last rites to Tom Costigan. The ritual for the dying, not the dead. It's not certain when the soul leaves the body. It could be hours after . . . after the heart— Eddie, my throat is very dry." He put his hand to his throat as if to confirm the fact.

I said, "Rye and ginger?"

He said, "That'll do fine. Just a wee drop, Eddie, just a wee drop for my throat."

My kitchen was an alcove off the living room. He continued talking while I assembled his drink.

"It was a terrible sight. The blood and the mess. I never saw anyone so . . . They say priests lead sheltered lives. Oh, we *hear* things that would . . . that would make Satan blush. But we don't *see* such savage things as—"

I said, "I was there, Frank. I saw him."

I gave him his drink, and he said, "God will reward you."

I shrugged, thinking that if God knew I gave whiskey to a whiskey priest, He'd add a hundred thousand days to my time in Purgatory. I saluted the priest with my own drink of apple juice and seltzer, knowing that it looked like a highball. Father Frank always asserted that he didn't like to drink alone. We all kid ourselves, even priests.

He gabbed on, and I gave up trying to follow his words, grunting now and then to show that I was still there. He said, "But sometimes a person can't make restitution. He has to try to make up, make up for it in other ways." He sipped from his glass daintily.

"Right," I said.

"They say that the men who dropped the bomb on Hiroshima never got over it. They couldn't make restitution, you see."

I grunted.

"I'm talking about penance," he said. "No matter how rig— No matter how rigorous it is, it can't, it can't atone for creating a monster."

He had pretty well demolished his drink with rapid-fire sips, and I was determined not to give him another. I had come to believe that the main reason Frank Garvin persisted in visiting me was that I was the last person in the parish who still fed him booze.

"Monster," I said, prompting him.

"That's what it is, Eddie." His voice quavered with emotion. "He's a thief, and I'm afraid he always will be. It's sad, very sad. I keep hoping that God will give him strength, but he's a weak man. I know about weakness, Eddie. I'm an expert on weakness, so to speak."

He stared at me as though he had lost his train of thought.

I said, "You were talking about a thief."

"Yes . . . yes, he always promises to make restitution, but I'm afraid he doesn't always do that. And he comes back and confesses he's stolen something else. And he promises to give it back. Again. And I give him absolution. You see, he needs the absolution, that's what he needs, and I say maybe he really means it this time—"

Suddenly, I was wide awake and listening carefully. The realization broke through my numb skull that my friend Frank Garvin was drunkenly committing what had to be a grave sin in his own eyes. He was breaking the seal of the confessional and talking about an actual penitent, apparently a habitual thief, whose latest theft had brought agony to the priest.

I wondered if I should listen, and, still wondering, I said, "What did he steal this time?"

He looked at me in shock. "You know better than to ask that, Eddie . . . ," he said. "What goes on in the confessional is completely confi . . . confidential."

"Sorry," I said. "Let me put some fresh ice in your glass."

He looked down at his empty glass. "I really shouldn't," he said. "But all right, just one more."

I made him another drink.

"Bless you, Eddie," he said, moving the burden of benediction from God to himself. Then he said, "I never realized there were so many Arabs in the neighborhood."

"More Latins and Asians," I said. "The Irish and Italians are moving out to the suburbs."

"These were Arabs."

"Who were?"

"The ones he stole from."

"Oh."

"He didn't take the money; it was all foreign. I mean, he took the American money, but not the foreign money. He didn't know if he could cash it in."

"Not much of a haul."

"So he took the box. It looked valuable."

I grunted.

"It wasn't big, but it was heavy, he said. Like it was made of lead." He was staring at the wall behind me with a look on his face that made me wonder if he was seeing green snakes writhing on it.

I said, "Was that the monster, Frank?"

He shook himself and said, "I'm talking too much. It's one of my faults."

"I wouldn't say that," I murmured.

Now his gaze was fixed on the glass he held with both hands, and his voice was so faint I could hardly hear him. "There's no such thing as an unforgivable sin. That's what I always thought. So long as there was true repentance and . . . and restitution."

"But in this case, he couldn't give it back," I said.

He squirmed. "In this case restitution might be worse. . . . Oh, all those poor, innocent people killed! The women and the babies and the screams of pain." He stopped talking, and started shaking his head as if to rid himself of some unbearable sights and sounds.

"Restitution might be worse," I said.

"Well, he couldn't, of course," he said after a moment. "He had already passed it on. He sold it for thirty dollars. Thirty pieces of silver. And he no longer had the money."

He swirled the liquor in his glass. "They call this demon rum, and that's what it is. He's no worse than me, Eddie. He drank it away. No, no, no, no, he isn't a Judas by any means, not at all. He's just a thief. The good thief, I like to think. I hope he turns out to be the good thief. He was repentant; that's a good sign. And he was something else, Eddie. He was frightened. He was trembling, poor man. Maybe his fright is good. Maybe now . . ." He stopped talking, and seemed lost in bleak thoughts.

"Frightened of the monster?" I said.

"That, too," the priest said. "He didn't know what it was until he sold it. It was just a heavy box. A heavy box. And then . . ." The drink slipped from his hands and spilled on the rug. He began to blink slowly.

I said, "Come on, Frank, I'll walk you home."

I put on my shoes, feeling that my hundred thousand days of Purgatory were starting.

The only way I could walk him back to the rectory was to drape his arm across my shoulders and practically carry him that way. It didn't do my damn shoulder wound any good.

Luckily, the sidewalks were deserted.

In front of the rectory, he said, "Them, Eddie. Not the monster. Them!"

If the box was stolen from Arab terrorists, I could understand the fear. I found myself sympathizing quite deeply with Father Garvin's "good thief."

"Did you give him absolution, Frank?"

"Abso . . . absolutely," he said.

At the door, I delivered him into the hands of the silent, grim-faced pastor, who nodded to me curtly and closed the door.

I stared at it dumbly for a minute, then went home.

6

The photograph showed me being helped—shoved—into the patrol car by a policeman. I looked like an arrested felon. The photo was on the front page of the *News*. The *Post* had somehow acquired a police photo of the blasted body. Even the *Times* had the story on page one. Surprisingly for the *Times*, however, it identified me as Edward Casey. Under the circumstances, I liked being Edward Casey.

To avoid the well-meaning questions of neighbors, I slipped out the back entrance of my apartment building.

Mullen's Funeral Parlor occupied the ground and first floors of two adjoining town houses on a street that was in the process of being reclaimed from slumhood by Yuppie families with enough dough to do it. I had once needled Hugh Mullen at Philbin's by asking him why he still called his place a "parlor" when every other last-sleep salon in the city was either a "home" or a "chapel."

"Because, my lad," he said, "it was the Mullen family's parlor before I converted the buildings. And because all good Irish wakes are held in a parlor, not in a—God forbid—a *chapel*. And it's what my father's place was called in the old country, and what was good enough for him is good enough for me. But you wouldn't understand, would you, Eddie?"

I understood the allusion to my less-than-complete Irish heritage. I said, "Too bad your old man emigrated, Hughie. You'd be doing land-office business in Northern Ireland these days, shoving stiffs into the old sod as fast as the British can shoot them down."

"Never you worry about the Brits," he said. "They'll be getting theirs with compound interest."

"When? Judgment Day?"

"Soon, laddie, soon," he said.

Mullen wasn't there at nine o'clock that Saturday morning. I left the clothes with his embalmer, Malcolm Something, a cadaverous man who was perpetually and beatifically half-bombed, even when taking up the collection at Sunday mass. "It's a terrible thing," the embalmer said, and I agreed.

"Would you care to see the remains?"

"Thanks, no," I said. "I've already seen them."

I went back home, tried to reach Alice by phone, and got a busy signal. Then I realized that every nut in the city and everyone who had ever been an acquaintance of Costigan's would be calling the bereaved daughter to offer condolences and conspire to drive her insane. I sighed and went on over there. I got through a small crowd on the sidewalk, and was allowed to enter by a uniformed cop stationed on the stoop.

Alice was standing in the middle of her living room, and there was already a demented look in her eyes. The phone was ringing.

I put my arms around her, and said, "Go do what you have to do. I'll take care of the phone."

She slumped in my arms. "The tintinnabulation of the bells has put bats in my belfry," she said. "How's your shoulder?"

"Which one?" I asked, and moved to answer the phone.

I manned the phone for most of the day. Some of the

calls were from distant relatives, phoning from places like Boston, Scranton, Pittsburgh, and San Diego, many of whom planned to descend on Mullen's Funeral Parlor and stay for the funeral Mass on Tuesday. One call came from the attorney general, the same man who had forced Costigan's retirement. Another came from the White House. I put Alice on to hear the words of the President, and they were very gracious words indeed, except that he referred to her father as "Tim" Costigan. But for the most part, the calls were from cranks and semicranks, and I developed a routine of answering, "It's very thoughtful of you to call, thank you," then hanging up.

The first night of Costigan's wake was an occasion comparable to the opening of a new discotheque. The mayor put in an appearance along with his police commissioner, followed by their army of political reporters, which clashed with the army of general-assignment reporters covering crime in the city. Democratic politicians from as far away as Canarsie swarmed like termites at spring roll call. And then there were the mourners, few of whom mourned, for few had had real affection for the man. They were there for the Irish wake.

I tried to save Alice from the ordeal of listening to all the painful malarkey that came so easily from the mouths of these people, but she refused to take refuge in a back room away from the crush. "I owe it to Da," she said, and, taking a position near the casket, submitted to the sanctimonious onslaught. Mercifully, the viewing hours were limited to 7 to 9 P.M. They were the longest two hours of my life, but Alice remained graciously attentive throughout the steamy session.

The mayor stepped on my toe, and the tide of torturers swept me away from Alice and temporarily brought me to rest among the cartoonists. Mort Laser said, "Tell Alice we think it was a shitty thing that happened to her father." And Bud Hicks said, "Damned shitty."

Helen Hills was choked with emotion. "He danced with me," she said. "And now this. Gone so quickly. It makes you think."

David Glass had the tight look of someone who was about to burst into tears. "Tell her we're sorry for her trouble, Father," he said.

It sounded like an Irish grouping of words to me, and I peered at him, wondering whether someone named Glass could really be Irish.

Helen Hills was saying, "Of course, he danced with his hand on my ass, and he was looking down my dress all the time, and he wasn't a very good dancer . . ."

Then I was being moved toward the bier and found myself gazing down at the pale visage of Tom Costigan, which looked up at me disdainfully even though his eyes were closed. Before opening the doors to the crowd, Hugh Mullen, Alice, and I had stood here and debated whether to have the casket open or closed. I was ambivalent on the subject of wakes. On the one hand, I thought the institution was barbaric, particularly since the departed usually bore little resemblance to his former vital self and, if he were aware of what was being done to him, wouldn't want to be caught dead looking like that. On the other hand, well, one couldn't very well say good-bye to a closed casket or give it a last kiss on the forehead. In this instance, since I couldn't think of anyone wishing to give Tom Costigan a last kiss, and considering the vicious gash on his cheek, I would have voted for closing the lid. But Mullen and Alice decided to leave it open, perhaps on the theory that the gash was a mark of honor for his lifelong fight against organized crime.

So I gazed down at what was left of Costigan, noting that none of the carnage done to his body was visible. The rosary beads entwined in his hands were Mullen's doing; I hadn't given them a thought when I was gathering his laying-out garments. Abruptly, I looked away. The thought of what lay below the double-breasted suit brought back Joseph Heller's too-vivid scene in *Catch 22* of the young airman unzipping his flying suit and rezipping it quickly to hold in his blasted entrails.

I stepped back, bumped into someone, turned to apologize, and found myself facing Max Abel.

"Sorry about that, Max," I said. "A little while ago, I was stepped on by the mayor. How about that?"

"What an honor," he said.

He was being buffeted from the rear and from either side by bulky individuals, and he was sweating.

I said, "Mullen has a room upstairs where—"

"I can't stay, Eddie," he said. "But there's something I want to talk to you about. A contributor. Something you ought to know. Could you drop by my place tomorrow afternoon?"

"Sure. Any time."

"Make it three."

I said okay, and then we were separated.

My boss, Chuck Godbold, bless him, was talking pompously to the mayor, who was obviously trying to head for the door. As I say, I really loved Chuck, but somehow the presence of important people gave him an uncontrollable urge to appear important, too.

When he thudded into me, I asked him if our esteemed publisher was coming, and he said that unfortunately Horace Hawthorne had a prior engagement at the opening of an animal sanctuary in Westchester County.

In a lugubrious tone, he said, "We've lost a contributor."

I said, "That's one way of looking at it."

I found myself near the casket once again, oppressed by the tiers of flowers. I noted that the most gigantic basket of all came from Joey Gargano, and one of the smallest from J. P. Cosgrove. Gargano's card read: "I remember the good times. So long, Joey." I was bumped from the rear into the flowers, and suddenly I needed a drink.

I managed to squeeze near Alice and mutter, "I'm going upstairs for a minute. Are you okay?"

She said, "Thank you so much," and I wasn't sure she was talking to me or the red-faced fat man who had captured her hand in both of his. I made it to the staircase. Halfway up, I glanced down at the mass of people and was struck by the number of bald heads, a beach of rounded stones.

In the hospitality room upstairs, about a dozen people of Irish extraction were doing some serious drinking. At this early stage, the tone was sullen, morose. I knew most of them by sight. Gert, the raucous barfly from Philbin's, was on the edge of weeping. When she saw me, she said, "Oh, my heart! And him such a fine man and a good father! I never drank to a better man, Eddie. He was better than all of us put together."

I said, "It's very thoughtful of you to say that, Gert," and dodged the wet kiss she was trying to plant on me.

The only ones who appeared to be in good spirits were Brendan Power and Honor O'Toole, who sat in a corner, talking in low voices, suppressing laughs. Brendan mumbled something to her; she looked at me and heaved with silent laughter. They were like kids in church, except that they had drinks in their hands and I was the butt of their joke.

Hugh Mullen said solemnly, "What'll it be, Eddie?" and I wasn't thirsty anymore.

I said, "Does this go on Alice's bill?"

"Now, now, you needn't worry about that," he said, moving away from me. "Just tell Malcolm what you want."

I looked at the embalmer, now dressed in funereal black. I wondered what he would do if I asked for a Bloody Mary.

I went back down to the first floor, where Father Frank Garvin was leading the group in the rosary. He was doing it badly; at one point, he stumbled over the sequence of words in the Lord's Prayer.

At nine, I began the job of easing the lingering guests out of the funeral parlor. Alice had at last found a seat on a camp chair, but she was surrounded by four clucking biddies. I took them gallantly by the arm, each in turn, and escorted them to the door. "Tom Costigan would greatly appreciate your going to the six-thirty Mass and offering it up for the repose of his soul," I told them. They promised they would.

At nine-thirty, Alice and I gazed once again at her father. "He liked ceremony, Eddie, but not this," she said. "When Mother died, he asked the priest to say the funeral Mass in Latin—it was a young priest—and the priest said, 'I'd like to, Mr. Costigan, but I don't know the Latin.' Da thought that was very sad. He said he had lived too long to see the beauty go out of the church. He didn't like the Mass in English and the people on cue shaking the hands of the people around them like they were at a convention. That wasn't ceremony, he said, that was baloney. . . . He was old-fashioned, and that's not bad. He didn't deserve this."

She gripped my arm, and we turned to leave. She stopped, reached behind the flowers, and pulled out her briefcase.

"*Here?*" I said. "You thought you might have a chance to correct papers *here*?"

She blushed. "Just force of habit," she said.

We walked slowly, all nervous energy drained. The breeze from the northwest was gloriously soothing as it dried the perspiration on our bodies. We talked about the weather.

"Do you think the hurricane will hit us?" she asked idly.

I assured her that the Democratic Party wouldn't let it.

Ninth Avenue was remarkably dead for a Saturday night. All the action was on Eighth. We turned into her street. Dead. Up the stoop and into the downstairs hallway. We had remembered to leave on a light. What we saw stopped us cold. The umbrellas from the stand were scattered about, the mirrored hatrack on the wall was askew, and the drawer in the table below it gaped open and empty.

"Shit, I never gave it a thought," I said. It was part of New York City wisdom I had learned as a child that burglars were avid readers of the obituary columns. When the hours of a wake were given, that meant that the home of the deceased would be empty during those hours nine times out of ten, and could be cleaned out of valuables at a leisurely pace. Easy pickins. "We better take a look," I said.

She followed me from room to room silently. Furniture was overturned, drawers pulled out and their contents scattered, and pictures taken from the walls, even the reproduction of Da Vinci's "Last Supper" in Costigan's dining room. His bedroom on the third floor was a shambles. But the worst havoc was wrought in his office area, where file cabinets were emptied on the floor and the drawers of his desk shattered as if tossed in angry frustration against the wall. The whole house had been ransacked, but only here was there evidence of malicious destruction. The Selectric II typewriter, which Tom had loved, was on the floor, obviously beyond repair.

I mounted the stairs to Alice's apartment. She lagged behind. Here we found the same disarray: furniture overturned, drawers opened, rugs flipped over, canisters in the kitchen spilled, the mattress thrown off her bed.

Alice walked as if her bones ached, and came to rest against the overturned sofa. Her face was the mask of tragedy.

"Are you okay?" I asked.

She didn't reply.

I righted an easy chair, went to her, and took her by the shoulders. "Sit," I said.

She clung to me, her face in my left shoulder. I moved her to my right shoulder. "At least nothing's ruined," I said. She continued to cling to me, breathing slowly.

I forced a light tone. "What can I give you?" I said. "Tea and sympathy? Scotch on the rocks?"

"Saki."

"What?"

"What I could use now," she said into my shoulder, "is a large quantity of hot saki." She shivered.

I said, "Hot saki coming up," and I sat her down in the chair. Remembering that Costigan had a bottle of port wine downstairs, I got it and gave her some in a wineglass. "Sorry, no saki," I said. "But my father always said, 'Any port in a storm.'"

"Oh, Eddie," she said with a little groan.

I righted the sofa and sat on it. Then I jumped up, went to the phone, and got a message through to Lieutenant Fred Ferrante. I returned to the sofa, happy to see that she had drunk some wine. Her face was still deathly pale, however.

I said, "Did you see the money on the floor?"

She looked at me with dead eyes.

"And the silverware?" I said.

She held the wineglass cupped in her two hands.

I said, "Can you stand another go-round with the police?"

She shrugged. At least, it was a response.

I said, "I want you to sleep at my place tonight."

She squirmed. "No," she said.

I studied her, and realized she was in no condition to walk the few blocks to my apartment. I went to her bedroom, put the mattress back on the bed, straightened the sheets and thin blanket, and went back to her. She had finished the wine.

I said, "In a few minutes we're going to be hip-deep in cops. Let me handle them. I'm going to put you to bed."

She frowned, but let me lead her to the bedroom and undress her. I put on her shortie pajamas. I said, "Go peepee," and she did. I put her in bed and pulled the sheet and blanket over her. She clung to my hand. I lay down alongside her on top of the covers. I said, "Did you ever bundle with a feller before?" She shook her head. After a while, she went to sleep.

* * *

Two hours later, Lieutenant Ferrante came back upstairs and sat down in the chair opposite me. The tremors had started after I had left Alice's bed and gone downstairs to open the door for the police. I had led them on a quick survey of the trashed rooms, winding up outside Alice's bedroom, where I had asked them to please not disturb her.

Then I had sat on the slashed sofa while they went about their chores in the rest of the house. It was at that point that the reaction had set in. After thirty-five years of a nonviolent existence, I was in the eye of a hurricane of violence. With no more duties of my own to distract me, my nerve endings had started to twitch.

So I had said to myself, "This calls for a very large Scotch on the rocks," and myself had agreed. Thus I had started sedating my craven nerves.

I said to Ferrante, "Scotch on the rocks. Want one?"

He let his shoulders slump. "Yeah, why not?"

After I handed him a generous pouring of Costigan's booze, I said, "It's not a burglary, is it?"

He shook his head. "They didn't even try to make it look like one." He took a bit of the drink and made a sound of satisfaction. "So this is an Irish wake," he said.

"I wouldn't know," I said.

"Have you had any further thoughts on what they were looking for?"

"The same thing you were looking for at the syndicate—something they don't want published."

"You're a big help, Carey. Any idea what it might be?"

"God knows," I said. "Whatever it was, it looks like they didn't find it."

"How so?"

"They searched every room in the house. Seems to me, if they had found it, they would have stopped and not searched the rest."

"Unless it was the last room they came to."

"Possible," I admitted. "Do you think it was the Mafia?"

"Possible," he said, echoing me. "But not likely. I don't like to brag about my paisanos, but they're more efficient than this. And if they didn't find it, they'd burn the house down just to make sure it was destroyed."

"At least they won't come back," I said. When he didn't respond, I added, "Will they?"

He shrugged. "I'm putting a man downstairs out front, and another on the roof. Miss Costigan will be safe tonight."

"Why on the roof?"

"That's how they came in."

"Through the hatchway?"

"Costigan didn't latch it very well. They used a crowbar."

"You think there's a possibility they'll come back."

He sighed. "I told you they're very thorough. They might want to ask questions of people who were close to Costigan's work."

"Meaning Alice and myself."

"Possible," he said. "I don't have a man to put on you. Go straight home and lock yourself in, hear?"

"Sure," I said.

But I didn't go straight home. I was all wound up again. I had to walk it off.

Before I left, I said, "Do you think it could be Arabs?"

"I don't know from Arabs," Ferrante said. "Why do you mention them?"

"Just a thought," I replied. "They seem to love to blow things up."

He rubbed his face. "There's no organization of Arab terrorists in this country that I know of, thank God. Do you think Costigan had a line on one?"

"I was just wondering," I said.

Then I left.

7

When you have a sedentary job and you live in Manhattan, you have to program some exercise into your daily routine or you'll wind up like me, overweight and soft. Working out at home—push-ups, weights, exercycles, and such—seems narcissistic to me. Jogging is grim—did you ever see a jogger smile? And taking up a sport like tennis, golf, swimming, or squash becomes an expedition. My exercise is walking. I'm a very good walker, if I do say so.

I had had enough of Costigan's Scotch to get me high, but not enough to dispel the jitters. My mind had St. Vitus's dance. I had to keep going until the dance was over. Twelve-thirty Saturday night was not the best hour to stroll through Times Square looking like a hayseed; besides, what I needed was not stimulation but quietude. So I confined my peregrinations to the Hell's Kitchen area west of Eighth Avenue. There was no point in trying to organize my thoughts. I just walked. Up to Fifty-ninth Street, across to Twelfth Avenue, down past the deserted docks and the dank smell of the river, down to Thirty-seventh or Thirty-eighth Street, I forget which, and back toward home.

This was my adopted neighborhood—seedy, smelly, clangorous with trucking in the daytime and eerily quiet at night, inhabited by the poor of every nationality—and I loved it. Incidentally, it was no longer called Hell's Kitchen. It was now called Clinton by the uplifters, la-di-da. The Port Authority had an exhibit devoted to the history of the area, under one of the ramps to the Bus Terminal. It included a blowup of a *New York Times* story, dated September 22, 1881. At that time, the area was known variously as "The Barracks," "The House of Blazes," "Battle Row," and "Sebastopol," in addition to "Hell's Kitchen." The story described the neighborhood thus:

> The entire locality is probably the lowest and filthiest in the city, a locality where law and order are openly defied, where might makes right, and depravity revels riotously in squalor and reeking filth.

I mused on this while my mind shifted slowly down to a quiet idle, and I was ready for bed. I was walking along one of the lowest and filthiest blocks of small manufacturing plants and warehouses, dark and deserted, where no riotous revelry was going on as far as I could see, when far ahead of me two human figures straightened and emerged from what only a moment before had appeared to be only a large pile of trash.

In the dim light, all I could note was that one was tall and thin and the other of average height and stocky. They walked quickly away from me and disappeared around the corner of Eleventh Avenue.

I mentally shrugged. I was in no mood to be confronted by two nocturnal scavengers who seemed to be out of luck since they had departed empty-handed. I kept walking, thinking that the two had emerged from the pile rather like gophers from their hole, remembering that the area had once been ruled by a criminal gang called the Gophers, which had eventually spawned the notorious Owen Madden. I trudged on, making little noise in my rubber-soled shoes.

The trash pile slopped over on the sidewalk and, at first glance, held nothing salvageable, just chunks of plasterboard, segments of rusted-through piping, empty cans, splintered beams and planks, soiled rags, and God knows what else. And a pair of shoes. Not work shoes. Not the ragged discards of a wino. But Hush Puppies, with tassles. The rhythm of my walking carried me beyond the pile before my mind registered what my eyes had seen in the darkness: a body attached to the shoes.

I didn't want to go back, but I did. The brown-and-yellow pattern of the plaid trousers had looked familiar. Even before I saw the face, I had a terrible premonition. I forced myself to inch closer, and bent over to see.

Danny Dunn. The gunsel lying on his back, staring up at the opaque sky. His hands clutching his throat as if there was something wrong with it, and he was having trouble breathing.

I reached down, shook his arm, and said, "Danny."

The hand came away from the throat, and I had a glimpse of what the trouble was. The whole forward part of his neck gaped open and glistened wetly in the darkness.

I said something like, "Oh, shit, Danny!" and felt myself falling on top of him. In horror, my hand reached out, found something solid—a beam, I think—to stop my fall, and I was able to stagger back.

I think I said the same thing a number of times: "Oh, shit, Danny." Then I moved away on rubbery legs.

I have no clear recollection of how I got to Philbin's Pub.

I stared at the jigger of Hennessey's, wondering if my stomach would reject it.

Lieutenant Fred Ferrante sat beside me, giving me a

chance to get strength back in my limbs for the walk back to Danny Dunn's last resting place and a reenactment of my movements.

He said, "You seem to be a lightning rod for violence, Carey." He said it sympathetically.

All the regulars were there when I careened in and asked to use the phone. The wake that had started so glumly at the funeral parlor was now going full blast—with Brendan speaking melodiously, Honor chirping counterpoint, Gert cackling, Mullen arguing, and Billy Philbin leaning on the bar with his massive arms and silently watching it all.

They quieted when they heard my end of the phone conversation, and then made me repeat my story. They sat me on a barstool; Philbin provided the brandy and Gert delivered a bibulous eulogy. "Oh, my heart! Is there no end to it! And him such a gentle little guy, he wouldn't hurt a fly! The poor little son of a bitch, he may have been a thief, but he never—"

"A good thief," I said. That started a discussion of whether Danny Dunn was a good thief or not, with most of them concluding that he wasn't really very good at his chosen profession. They all sympathized with me, but no one touched me.

I stared at the jigger and concentrated on pacifying my stomach.

Later, I said to Ferrante, "Why are you here? I thought you were only interested in organized crime."

"I'm interested in a lot of things," he said.

"Do you think this was a gang killing?"

"Possible," he said.

In a kill-or-cure motion, I downed the brandy. When the rumpus it caused subsided, it stayed down.

Ferrante got me on my feet and started toward the door. He said, "I want you to focus on the two men you saw. Try to remember everything about them."

I was glad to get out of there. I disliked being the

center of attention, particularly when my face was green and I was one spasm away from throwing up. I still felt like walking, so we walked, with the police car following.

I said to Ferrante, "I just discovered something."

"What's that?" he said.

"I don't like cognac. It tastes like it was distilled in a rusted tin can."

"*De gustibus*," the lieutenant said. "What about those two jokers?"

"I've told you all I can. I thought they were ragpickers. But even if I thought they were worth looking at, I couldn't have seen any more than I did."

"Fat and Skinny had a race," Ferrante said.

"No, maybe five nine and stocky. The other guy maybe six two and, well, slender. That's it."

"How about their hair?"

"What about their hair?"

"Like, did either of them have an Afro?"

I called their silhouettes back into my mind. "No, I'd say they were white guys."

"Why do you say that?"

"They walked like white guys."

"How do white guys walk?"

"Like we're doing right now, for God's sake."

"No need to lose your temper. So the probability is, they were male Caucasians. Are you sure they were male?"

"A woman doesn't walk like they did."

"Now we're getting somewhere," Ferrante said, but I couldn't detect any sarcasm in his voice.

I said, "I think you're right, Lieutenant. This killing is in your bailiwick."

"Organized crime?"

"I don't know about that," I said. "But if you belong on the Costigan case, you belong on this one." I told him about the message the gunsel had given me for Tom Costigan.

"One of Costigan's snitches?"

"I think so," I said. "I also think that Danny Dunn went to confession."

Ferrante said, "The extent of your knowledge amazes me."

"It's not knowledge, it's only hearsay and guesswork. And you'll never be able to check it out, because you can't question a priest about what went on in the confessional. And he's not supposed to tell you even if you fit him with thumbscrews. And if he does tell you, whether freely or not, he can't testify for you in a court of law. Not only that, the priest with loose lips will sink straight to hell. Unless, of course, he himself goes to confession, gets absolution and—"

"Enough already," Ferrante said. "You sound like you're reciting a Miranda for priests. I get the point." He nodded toward an empty packing crate. "Let's sit down here a moment."

We sat. It felt good to get off my feet. My mind glazed over.

Ferrante said, "Danny Dunn told you he went to confession?"

"No."

"The priest did."

"In a way," I said. "I won't mention the name of the priest. That wouldn't be baseball—"

"Baseball?"

"I'm Americanizing the English expression."

"Tell it straight, damn it!"

My recollection of Father Frank Garvin's disjointed chatter was fuzzy, to say the least. "Okay," I said. "The priest came to my home the other night—"

"What night?"

My mind fumbled with the sequence of days and nights. "My God, it was only last night. Seems like last week."

His eyes told me to go on.

"The poor guy was already three sheets to the wind.

Not to put too nice a point on it—I like that—not to put too nice a point on it, this priest is an alcoholic. He was in an agitated state—really spooked, if you know what I mean—and he needed another drink very badly."

"So you gave him one."

"So I gave him one. I figured he had to talk to someone about what was on his mind or he'd go off his rocker, really off. He gabbed away and wasn't making much sense, and I just nodded and tuned him out. I was tired. He talked about confession, and whether sins could be unforgivable, and about the theft of something he called a 'monster.' Then he was talking about a *particular* penitent, and I gave him another drink."

"Danny Dunn?"

"He didn't mention a name; he was scrupulous about that. And I never thought of Dunn until tonight, although the priest did indicate that the sinner was a habitual thief. But I never—"

"So Dunn stole a monster."

"From Arabs."

"Arabs?"

"He was specific on that, strangely enough. Do you have a line on any organized band of Arab criminals?"

Ferrante shook his head. "There are some cuckoos, religious nuts who'll blow you up for Allah, or stick a knife in you for being sympathetic to Israel. But no large group of them that can be considered a major danger to us."

"How about the PLO or one of those fanatical factions in Lebanon?"

Ferrante shrugged. "Possible," he said. "Whatever they do over there, they haven't caused any trouble here."

I said, "Could be the priest had it all wrong, and just imagined that Dunn went to him to confession."

"No, let's assume that he did. Did your priest say what this monster was?"

"No, just that it was a box. A heavy box."

"No idea what was in it?"

"Not when he took it, but it seems that the thief found out when he passed it on to somebody else—a fence or whoever. And apparently, what he found out scared the hell out of him. And he must have told the priest, because the good father was trembling not only from the booze but from *fear*. I'll swear to that, he was scared to death. That's why he had to talk about it, to exorcise the monster. At least, that's the way I figure it."

"And you don't know who he passed it on to?"

"No."

"A box. A heavy box. What was it made of?"

"I don't know."

"What size? Was it bigger than a breadbox?"

"I don't know."

"That's it? That's all you have?"

"Such as it is."

Ferrante studied me for a moment. "So what we have is this," he said. "A man, Tom Costigan, who is an enemy of all organized crime groups in the country, is blown to bits by a fragmentation grenade. We figure it can only have been done by one of the outfits he was investigating, but we have no idea which one. Then one of his snitches— You have no idea what he was snitching to Costigan about?"

"Not really," I said. "He possibly fed him some material on Joey Gargano, but I don't know."

"Okay, then one of his informants has his throat cut from ear to ear and is thrown on a trash heap. Before that, the informant tells a priest he has stolen something frightening from some Arabs—we don't know what it was—and that he passed it on. Did he say he sold it? Did he get money for it?"

"Yes, he did. He got thirty bucks."

"He sold it for thirty bucks to someone else. We don't know who."

"And he can't get it back."

"He said that?"

"The priest said he couldn't make restitution. And he had already spent the dough."

Ferrante was silent for a moment. "So there we are," he said. "I'd say the two murders are definitely connected, even though the MOs are different. Nobody says a killer has to use the same weapon each time."

I said, "So there we are. Nowhere."

"No," Ferrante said. "This time we have a witness and a partial description of two of the killers. Male Caucasians. We also know they're looking for something and haven't found it. We know two more things. First, it's a good bet they'll keep on looking."

When he was silent for a minute, I said, "What's the other thing?"

"If they find out about the witness, they'll try to kill again."

To show you the state of my mind, the exhaustion, the near-stupor I was in, the near-schizophrenic split between reality—the empty crate I was sitting on—and the unreality of the violent deaths of those around me, I jumped to my feet and laughed. It just seemed tremendously funny to me. I said, "Great! That's simply great, Lieutenant."

Ferrante stood up. "What's so funny?"

Abruptly, I was sober. "Nothing," I said. "It's just that . . . well, nothing." I used to laugh at horror movies. Now I was in one.

Ferrante said he would keep my name out of the papers and black out any mention of the two men seen leaving the scene of the latest murder. He said that a policeman would stay in my apartment overnight. I was too tired to argue.

The next morning I went to Mass for the first time in more than a year. The cop went with me.

8

To paraphrase, you can take the boy out of the seminary, but you can't take the seminary out of the boy. Frankly, my body of beliefs was in dusty disarray as a result of the benign neglect I had imposed on it, but the thought of being the target of killers, however incredible it was, raised the urge *causa mortis* to put my spiritual life in order, just in case.

The cop who took over at eight in the morning was a young, seemingly humorless guy named Saul. He was a darkish man with a long, lean face and quickness in his eyes. He went with me to the newsstand to get the Sunday papers and came back with me. Neither paper had any mention of last night's murder, only a rehash of Costigan's.

Saul and I had a breakfast of scrambled eggs, toast, and coffee.

I said, "Sorry, Saul, but I'm going to church."

He said, "Suddenly, I see a blinding light and my name is Paul. I'm going with you."

Cross out "humorless." I thought that was pretty funny.

We sat together in the far corner of the last pew, the way Western gunmen played blackjack with their backs to the wall. Nothing much happened. The pastor was a droner, seemingly fearful of arousing unseemly religious fervor. The embalmer passed the collection basket and I put in ten bucks, not as a bribe, damn it. At the point in the Mass when one is called on to demonstrate good will toward one's fellow parishioners, I saw Hugh Mullen shaking the hand of everyone he could reach. If there were a baby there, he would have kissed it.

Afterward, Saul said, "No offense, but that was the dullest sermon I ever heard."

I said, "Oh? Did somebody talk?"

He said, "May I make a suggestion?"

"Sure."

"You need Mahalia Jackson."

I said, "Write to the cardinal."

Under protest, he went with me to the Costigan house. There were stories in the papers of Hurricane Colleen battering Hatteras and possibly heading this way, but it was hard to believe. The air was clear that Sunday morning, and the sun was wonderfully warm on our shoulders. After sitting still for an hour in church, during which time I brooded without direction and did nothing about the disarray of my soul, I had to keep moving, moving, not frantically, simply restlessly.

"Out here, you're a target," Saul grumbled, scanning tenement windows and rooftops.

I said reasonably, "If they don't know where I'm going, or when, they can't very well set up an ambush, can they?" My dumb body, healthy and still comparatively young, was beginning to deny that death could be stalking me in the immediate present; maybe they'll get you in the other shoulder, it was telling me, but that's the worst-case scenario, so relax.

The cop on duty outside the Costigan house said, "There's a fat guy up there." So Saul insisted on going up to Alice's quarters with me to make sure the fat guy posed no threat.

Joey Gargano sat on the slashed sofa with a mug of coffee in his hand. Alice sat across from him. Her coffee was on the lamp table beside her.

Alice jumped up and peered at me with a worried look. "Are you all right?" she asked.

I said, "Right with Eversharp," a catchphrase from my childhood. She hugged me briefly.

Saul and Gargano were confronting each other.

"Up," Saul said.

Gargano said, "I've already been frisked."

"So we'll do it again," said Saul.

Gargano lumbered to his feet and walked with dignity to face the wall.

Alice said, "That won't be necessary, Officer."

Saul said, "He doesn't mind," and he ran his hands expertly over the tightly packed body.

Alice said, "Are you satisfied?"

Saul nodded to her gravely and said to me, "I'll be downstairs."

After he left, Alice said, "I'm sorry, Mr. Gargano."

Joey Gargano tried to smile. "I figured they do that to all friends of the Costigan family," he said. "Tom was a tough man." I thought he pulled Alice through her embarrassment very nicely. He resumed his seat on the sofa.

I noticed that most of the mess made by the searchers had been cleared up. After she brought me some coffee, I said, "You must have been up early."

"And you must have been up late," she said. "It must have been awful."

"How do you know?"

"That Lieutenant Ferrante was here."

I glanced dubiously at Gargano, then told the two of them of my surreal adventure on a deserted street of Sebastopol. Gargano questioned me closely about the two scavengers I had seen, then shook his head.

"Beats me," he said.

"Why the police guard?" Alice asked me.

"Dead men tell no tales, and all that," I said. "I was an eyewitness."

Joey said, "Tell us about the Arabs."

"What Arabs?"

He gave me a disgusted look, and I realized that a man in his position had eyes and ears in many places, including the police department. I had told only Ferrante about the Arabs, and while I doubted that Ferrante was Gargano's source, he surely wrote a report that was circulated and seen by the Mafia mole.

He continued to gaze at me until I recounted the night visit of the distressed priest, and also the gunsel's message to Tom Costigan. Alice followed my words with a shocked expression, and I realized she was hearing it for the first time.

Gargano said, "The poor little bastard stuck his hand in the fire, didn't he?" He said it sympathetically.

He put down his coffee and leaned forward with his elbows on his knees. "Listen. The reason I came here and imposed myself on Tom's girl—"

Alice started to protest, and he stopped her.

"I heard a story," he said. "Maybe it means something, and maybe it don't. The reason I heard it, one of the kids came around looking to buy a gun. Okay, here it is. Some bright college kids built themselves a bomb. This was out in the Midwest somewhere. They were into nuclear physics, and they built themselves a simple little atomic bomb. I understand it's pretty easy to do, once you know the proportions—something about a plug of uranium being shot into another plug of uranium—and that's it, you blow up the whole college. Little snot-nosed smartasses, that's what they were.

"Anyway, there was the bomb, and they didn't know what to do with it. Like building a boat in your basement—how the hell are you going to get it out? They had built this crazy thing, but they couldn't show it to their teacher, and they weren't about to explode it and blow themselves up. All they could do was take it apart again, but before they could, one of the kids grabbed it and ran off. The kid was from one of the Arab countries. The other kids were sure he brought it to New York, and they came after him. They figured they'd need a gun to persuade him to give it back. The people I'm acquainted with wouldn't sell to them."

"Of course not," I said.

He gave me a pained look. "Anyway, they didn't find the Arab kid, and they went back home. I imagine they did a lot of praying."

I said, "How come they blabbed about the bomb? I mean, what they did was a crime, and they wouldn't go around telling strangers about it."

"I know a guy who can make a deaf mute talk," he said. His placid face showed wonder at his friend's talent.

Alice said, "Is that the end of the story? An Arab kid brought a homemade bomb to New York, and nobody knows what happened to him or it?"

"Not exactly," Gargano said. "We know the kid went back to his own country."

"What country is that?"

"Lebanon."

"Good Lord!" Alice exclaimed. "He took an atomic bomb to Lebanon? *Lebanon!*"

Gargano shook his head. "No, he left it here."

My imagination was running ahead of him. "The kid was a terrorist, and he left it with an Arab terrorist group here in New York. But Ferrante said there was no—"

"Not terrorist," Gargano said. "Religious. The kid was religious, and he donated it to his religious cause."

"Same difference."

"Maybe."

I said, "The PLO is political, not religious."

"Right. This was a religious group."

"Which one?"

Gargano sighed. "It's hard to tell. I don't have a scorecard. They call themselves something like Friends of Allah or Allies of Allah or something."

"So some religious nuts who hate the U.S. have an atomic bomb in New York City. Great!"

Gargano sat back. "The last I know of it," he said slowly, "the bomb was in their cruddy headquarters on Eighth Avenue. That was a week ago. It may still be there, for all I know. And that's all I know, kiddies."

I rattled my head to clear it. "I hate to ask this question, Joey," I said, "but what's in it for you? You obviously spent a lot of manpower tracking the damn thing down. What was in it for you?"

He stared at me coldly. "Even people like me can be patriotic once in a while," he said. "Besides, I happen to live in New York, and I don't like the idea of one of those things in the hands of loonies near where I live."

"But you didn't tell the police," I said.

"We don't work that way," he said.

I started to retort. "Then how in hell were you going to—"

Alice interrupted me. "Don't you see what he's saying, Eddie? He's saying he doesn't think the Arab terrorists have it anymore. He thinks poor Danny Dunn stole it without knowing what it was."

"He put his hand in the fire," Gargano murmured.

I said, "But don't you think the Arabs might have gotten it back from him? In that case—"

Gargano wearily raised a hand. "What did Father Frank say? He said there could be no restitution because Dunn had sold it. No, it doesn't figure that the Arabs got it back."

"Then the Arabs must have killed him."

Gargano let his shoulders slump. "I don't think it's important who killed Danny Dunn," he said. "What's important is who killed this young lady's father, my friend Tom Costigan. From where I'm sitting, it doesn't figure to be Arabs. It figures to be the bozos who now have that little package of dynamite from the Midwest."

"And we don't know who they are," Alice said.

I said, "Only two people knew. The thief who stole it, and the man he told his story to."

"Father Garvin."

"Maybe him. No, I was thinking of Tom Costigan. And they're both dead."

We talked about that for a while. I said. "I'm beginning to believe that they deliberately planned to kill all three of us that first time, not just Tom. I mean his daughter and his editor. Who knew what he had told us?"

"And the search," Alice said. "They searched up here, even though it was obviously my quarters, not my father's. What were they looking for?"

That stumped us. Something the gunsel may or may not have passed on to Costigan. Perhaps only Costigan's notes on Dunn's information. Perhaps something more tangible.

When Gargano rose to his feet to leave, he said. "Don't build this up too big. We're only guessing it was the college kids' bomb that Danny stole." He gave Alice the embrace of an uncle. "I'll keep nosing around," he said.

After he left, Alice said, "Do you believe him?"

I said, "Yes."

"About the bomb?"

"I believe college kids could make one," I said. "The only hard part would be getting the materials, and for snot-nosed smartasses that wouldn't be too difficult."

"You really think that's what Danny Dunn stole?"

I made a face. "Knowing Dunn's talent for blundering, I'm ready to believe it. It's not just bad luck with him, it's a perverse gift. In 'The Lady or the Tiger,' he'd choose the tiger every time."

Despite what I said to Alice, I didn't really believe in the bomb's existence. It was too out of the ordinary, too bizarre. Even so, we agreed that the police ought to be told. I dialed Ferrante's number and left word for him to call me. My nerves were acting up again.

I helped Alice with her cleanup job, happy to be busy and not thinking. At one-thirty, we walked hand in hand around to Vinnie's for a lunch of Sicilian pizza and a glass of Chianti. Saul went with us. Joey Gargano wasn't there.

Afterward, we went for a little walk. Passing Philbin's, I saw that the usual crowd was there, Brendan Power emoting, apparently concocting an extemporaneous bit of verse that Honor O'Toole was inscribing on a piece of paper, Hugh Mullen grinning, Gert cackling. I shook my head, wondering that I had ever found this group of professional Irishers fascinating. A scrap of what Power was saying came out—"That's him all over"—followed by an explosion of laughter. I hoped that Alice hadn't heard it.

Some of her out-of-town relatives arrived at quarter to three. They were in town more for a visit to New York than to honor their murdered cousin, and were staying at the Sheraton Centre. I abandoned Alice to their unfeeling attentions and left.

"Come on, Saul," I said to my shadow. "We're going to the East Side to see how the other half lives."

"Why don't we just go home and hunker down," he said. "This moving around in the open is giving me the jitters."

"If Gary Cooper were like you," I said, "the West would never have been won. Come on."

Saul wanted to take a cab, but I wanted to walk. We walked crosstown through Times Square, somnolent in the midday light, through Rockefeller Center, populated only by tourists with cameras, and on up to the forbidding habitats of the rich and exclusive. The high that had been our weather for the past few days was now departing toward New England, and the sky was clouding up. We walked through the soupy air, and I felt good. Saul complained about so much walking, and I made some not-very-clever pleasantries about policemen's feet, and then we were there.

Max Abel's apartment building had a cavernous, marble-and-chrome lobby presided over by a spiffily uniformed black man who somehow reminded me of Orphan Annie's friend, Punjab. Perhaps it was the way he folded his arms across his massive chest, and the palatial Daddy Warbucks surroundings. When he spoke, his voice had the masterful resonance of James Earl Jones.

I gave him Max's name and my own, and he punched out Max's room number on the internal phone system. Even as we waited for a response, my false sense of well-being drained away from me and anxiety started nibbling.

The major-domo of the lobby said, "There's no answer, sir."

I stammered out an explanation that Mr. Abel had told me to come at three. I looked at my watch and saw that it was seven minutes after.

The man tried the intercom again. No response.

I had been in Max's apartment several times, and I pictured his body lying on the thick blue carpet of his living room. I remembered how he had looked at Costigan's wake, and I managed to say, "Something's happened to him."

Saul was peering closely at me. He shrugged, and said in a quiet tone, "Let's take a look."

I was in a cocoon. Time passed outside me. I walked. I was in the elevator. I walked with Saul and the majestic doorman to Max's apartment. When the man used a master key to open the door, I entered.

Max was not lying as I had pictured him on the living room floor, and my sense of foreboding turned to one of embarrassment. Suppose the reason Max didn't answer the in-house phone, I thought suddenly, was that he was otherwise occupied with one of his pliant admirers in that king-size bed of his? Imagine breaking in on that scene!

The doorman called Max's name. Nothing but silence. He looked at me questioningly.

I took a deep breath and caught the faint aroma of Max's cologne. His were not the typical bachelor's digs; he was a lover of women, and his furnishings were ornately French, which in my ignorance of decorating I took to be Louis the Fifteenth or something like that.

I marched to the hall leading to his bedroom and entered it. The silken sheets were rumpled. The bed had been slept in, but was now empty. No ribald tableaux today, thank God. I retreated into my cocoon.

Saul was ahead of me. It was he who opened the bathroom door. He froze. "Is that your friend?" he asked in a quiet voice.

I followed him into the bathroom.

The naked body of Max Abel rested peacefully in several feet of water in the sunken bathtub. His eyes were closed, and he could have been sleeping. The dominant blue color of the living room was carried over into here. The porcelain and tile were blue. The nappy carpeting was blue. Only the water was red, and the Gem safety razor blade on the floor beside the tub.

The black man caught me before I cracked my skull on the floor.

9

I was slumped in the leather chair in Max's study. I heard movements and men's voices in other areas of the apartment, but I was alone in here, at least for the moment, with essence of Max. I noted his shelves of books, his Tiffany lamp, his brown carpeting, glass-topped desk, Kaypro word processor and printer connected by an umbilical cord, cabinets of polished wood, files of floppy disks, and red flowers—I don't know what breed—near the window. There was a brown leather sofa opposite the chair I was in. My vision pulsated sickeningly, and I closed my eyes, determined never to open them again.

Max Abel was a man caught up in the wrong profession. He was a smart enough banker, but there was so much more to him than there was to his banking cohorts. What was it the old WASP families used to say? . . . If a son is too dumb to go into business or government, put him in banking. I don't know what put Max into banking. Probably the Jewish heritage of hedging against persecution. But his inclinations were more those of an artist or a poet. He was a Don Juan who, instead of using women, put himself at their disposal—gallantly. He was gallant, and now he was gone.

The leather of the sofa creaked, and a voice said, "Carey?"

I said, "Hello, Lieutenant. I thought this was your day off."

"It was," Ferrante said. "If it weren't for you, I'd be drinking a beer and watching the ballgame."

"Go on back home, for God's sake," I said. "Max had nothing to do with organized crime."

"Something the matter with your eyes?"

"No."

"I don't know if you've noticed it, but your eyes are closed."

"That's because I've come to like you," I said. "I don't want anything to happen to you."

The lieutenant sighed. "You just lost me."

I said, "I'm the reincarnation of Medusa. All she had to do was look at somebody, and they'd turn to stone. Maybe it's Evil Eye Fink I'm thinking of. I go around looking at people, and they wind up dead. I don't want to do that to you."

"You're not talking sense. I know you've had a shock—"

"I have this feeling," I said, "that if I hadn't looked at Max, he'd be in there soaping his armpits and singing. You've heard of Typhoid Mary—"

Ferrante said, "Okay, so you're a carrier of death. I believe it! Now tell me why you came here today."

The question forced me to concentrate on something besides the squirming of my conscience. I opened my eyes. Ferrante was dressed in a yellow T-shirt and pale-blue slacks. Shoved to the back of his head was a Met baseball cap.

I said, "Max asked me to drop by. There was something I should know about one of our contributors, he said."

"Contributors to what?"

"The syndicate. The *Herald-Courier* syndicate. We syndicate Max's personal-finance column, along with a couple of dozen other columns and cartoons to newspapers around the country, from the profound to the ridiculous.

Political punditry from the most eminent of all political pundits, Otto Walters, down to—"

"I get the picture," Ferrante said. "Which one was Abel talking about?"

"He didn't say. That's what he was going to tell me at three o'clock." Suddenly, I had to swallow, and I closed my eyes.

"When did he ask you to come here?"

"Last night. At the wake."

"Who else was around?"

"Well, there was the mayor, some district attorneys, and half the population of New York. It was a mob scene."

"So you don't know who might have overheard him."

"Right with Eversharp," I said.

After a while, I opened my eyes and saw that Ferrante was still sitting on the sofa, gazing at me.

I said, "What do you know about an Arab religious group called Friends of Allah or Allies of Allah or something like that?"

He said, "Not much, if they're the ones I'm thinking of. They're one of the factions who are killing off the population of Lebanon. Why do you ask?"

"They don't have the homemade atom bomb anymore," I said.

"Is that a fact?" he said.

"No, it's not a fact. It's conjecture."

Ferrante kept his gaze fixed on me.

I said, "I left word for you to call me."

"I know," he said.

"It's a story I can't verify," I said. "And I'd rather not tell you my source. Just take it for what it's worth." I gathered my wits sufficiently to tell him Gargano's account of the atomic contraption and the possible theft of it by the bad-luck gunsel, Danny Dunn.

Ferrante asked me a lot of questions until he was satisfied that he had gotten every scrap of information that was in my head. Then he said, "They don't call them atom bombs or atomic bombs anymore. They call them nuclear bombs or nuclear warheads. Are you sure he said 'atomic'?"

"Atomic," I confirmed. "I don't know beans about anything smaller than the head of a pin, but I think I remember that the difference is between fission and fusion. The atom bomb is fission, and the nuclear bomb is fusion, and I just exhausted my college physics, in which I got a C-minus. Bigger bang for the buck, and all that."

He was silent for a while. "Farfetched," he said.

"That's the word I was looking for," I said.

"But frightening."

"Yes. Makes it important to find Danny Dunn's heavy box. Do the police know where he generally took the things he stole? From his past record, I mean."

"Various places, most of them now out of business. One of them's still operating. The Lo Discount Outlet, run by an Oriental gentleman named Lo, down on Hudson Street. The burglary boys made a routine check of his inventory just last week. No heavy box reported. I'll have them check again."

I said, "What sort of a discount do you suppose you could get on a homemade atomic device? It's something every red-blooded terrorist should have."

"Okay," Ferrante said. "Now tell me who told you the story."

I said, "I'm a newspaperman, Lieutenant. I claim a privileged relationship under the First Amendment. You can't force me to divulge my source."

Ferrante smiled. "In the first place, you're not a newspaperman. In the second place, there's no such privilege under the First Amendment or any other amendment. And in the third place, I won't do anything to him in the first place. I just want to judge how much weight to give his story."

"Promise?"

"Cross my heart," he said.

So I told him about Joey Gargano. Joey hadn't pledged

me to secrecy, but I felt slightly treacherous all the same. "You promised not to hassle him," I said.

"It's still a promise," the lieutenant said. "He's used this method of sending us information before. The only question is whether he's blowing smoke in our eyes to cover his own involvement, or whether the story is straight."

"You mean he used me as a messenger boy?"

Ferrante nodded. "Don't feel hurt, Carey. You did a good job."

I closed my eyes and groaned. "Where does old Max fit in?" I asked.

"He probably doesn't," Ferrante said. "You said he looked sick the last couple of times you saw him. We've already checked with his doctor. He did have prostate trouble."

I opened my eyes and glared at him. "So you think he killed himself?"

"That's what it looks like."

I shook my head. "Max was not the type to commit suicide."

"Nobody is, until they get sick," Ferrante said.

"You found a note?"

"No. Not all suicides leave notes."

"Max would have."

A uniformed cop stuck his head in the door. "We're through here, Lieutenant," he said.

Ferrante stood up.

"That's it?" I asked in bewilderment.

"I guess so, Carey. Are you coming?"

I looked at my watch, amazed to see that it was five-thirty. "In a few minutes," I said wearily. "Let me just sit here with Max for a few minutes. I loved the old bastard."

The lieutenant asked solicitously if I was going to be all right. I assured him that I would.

Then I was alone in Max's study. After a period of silence, I found myself talking to him. I said, "The damn prostate couldn't have been that important, could it?"

Then I said, "There's more to pleasing women than giving them a patented Max Abel orgasm." I even laughed. "Listen to me, Max—the famous ladies' man, Ed Carey!"

I peered around the room. The only pieces of art were a small sculpture on the desk of a humorously elongated Don Quixote astride Rosinante, and a pale sketch of a female nude hanging on the wall, a Picasso print.

I said, "No, you didn't do it, did you, old friend?"

I got up from the chair and moved through the hush of the room. I came back to the Kaypro, the same breed of word processor I used in the office; I had even bought one for my personal use, only to find I had little use for it. If Max had written a suicide note, he would have done it on this, and then left the disk in plain sight on the desk for someone to find. The desk was clear. If his mind was in a turmoil, he might have absently filed it away.

I opened his file of floppy disks. The first one he had labeled "IRA." It sounded like the title of a book. The next five disks were labeled "ESTHETICS OF FINANCE," numbered one through five. Another book he was writing? I wouldn't have thought that finance had any esthetic aspects at all. There were other disks with titles that had no meaning for me.

I closed the file, then opened it again. The "Ira" intrigued me. If it were a short story of Max's, I wanted to read it. On the other hand, it might be a reference to a relative, his father or a brother perhaps, conceivably even a son. I knew nothing of his family, and had no idea of who should be notified of Max's death. I put the disk in one of his six- by nine-inch envelopes and stuffed it in my pocket. I started to leave.

I looked back at the room and felt desolated. I said, "May flights of happy female angels sing thee to thy rest."

I walked quickly through the shadowed living room and out of the apartment. The uniformed policeman in the hall looked at me in surprise.

I said, "Where's my shadow?"

"Who?"

"Saul. The cop who was with me."

"Oh, he went off duty at four," the policeman said.

"No one took his place?"

"Not that I know of, buddy."

I made a face and left. Either I was no longer in danger, or somebody goofed.

10

I was disconnected, a hulk standing with Alice near Costigan's bier and the banked flowers as strangers murmured condolences and remembrances of the living Tom, all of which washed over me like a tepid breeze. The Costigan relatives were squirts of cold air. Most of them tried to appear sincerely grief-stricken, and did a poor job of it. They were the hardest to take. The more honest ones spoke of their exciting day vacationing in Manhattan; none of them had had the thrill of popping in on a dead man in a bathtub, however.

The most obnoxious one was Cousin Agnes from St. Louis, an aggressive middle-aged woman who wouldn't shut up, even though she had some malformation in her speaking apparatus that gave her voice a rattling, grating timbre. She told Alice at length of her interest in genealogy, then tugged me aside and told me of her explorations into the Costigan ancestry. The assault on my ears by this woman was comparable to being in a steel mill. "And that makes us direct descendants of Brian Boru!" she screeched up at me.

I had a vague idea of who Brian Boru was, although I pictured him as a furry primitive only recently down from the trees. "You don't tell me," I said.

"But I do! The greatest king of them all, Brian Boru! What did you say your name was again?"

I said, "I forget," and for the moment it was true. Then I said, "Excuse me," and went to talk to Billy Philbin, the pub owner, even though I didn't particularly like him.

"Had to show up to pay my respects," Philbin mumbled, obviously ill at ease. "Only have a few minutes. Where's Tom Costigan's girl?"

My boss, Chuck Godbold, put in an appearance for the second straight night. His pale, round face was scowling, and glistening with sweat. "Someone is killing off our contributors," he said in such an aggrieved tone that I realized he regarded the deaths of Costigan and Abel as a direct attack on him and the syndicate.

I said, "Look on the bright side, boss. Maybe they'll take Cosgrove next."

He frowned his disapproval of my sorry joke and said, "We need someone quick to take Max's place. Who can we get? Someone with a name in family finance."

I said, "How about Jacqueline Onassis?"

He grinned in sudden glee, and as suddenly slipped back into a scowl. "We couldn't get her," he said.

I said, "By the way, I won't be in tomorrow."

He gripped my shoulder in sympathy. He said, "Take all the time you need. Sleep late. Don't come in until eleven or twelve."

"All day, Chuck," I said. "And Tuesday morning's the funeral."

He sighed noisily. "Think about a replacement for Max, and call me," he said.

"Okay."

"All that billing," he groaned.

I went upstairs to the hospitality room. No one was there. The liquor cabinet was locked. After a moment of thinking it over, I broke the cabinet open and poured myself three fingers of Scotch.

I slumped into a chair, and was surprised to find that I was crying. Real men don't cry, I said to myself. But what the hell, Tom Costigan never thought I was a real man. Neither did Max Abel. For different reasons. Tom was afraid I would screw his daughter, and Max was afraid I wouldn't. The question was, what did Alice think? We never said "I love you" to each other, and yet . . . and yet, son of a gun, we *did* love each other, and time was flitting past, and all we did was treat each other like buddies, touchy about sex.

I was on my second three fingers of Scotch when Hugh Mullen charged into the room with a black politician I didn't know. I could tell the man was a politician because even before we were introduced he strode over to me with a smile and a handshake.

I said, "Join the party, gentlemen!"

The politician laughed and said, "I hope you're referring to the right party, son."

Mullen said, "What the hell have you done to my cabinet?"

I explained to him in the most reasonable of tones, "Some misguided soul locked the damn thing, Hughie, and I took the liberty of opening it up. I knew you would approve."

His face got red, and his whole body seemed to inflate like a figure in the Macy's parade.

I said, "After all, it's an Irish wake, isn't it?"

Mullen said in a tight voice, "I'm asking you to leave. Mr. Wilson and I have a few things to discuss."

"Go right ahead," I said. "Don't mind me."

"In private," Mullen said.

I struggled to my feet. "I can take a hint," I said. "It's been a pleasure meeting you, Mr. Wilson." I finished my drink, spilling some of it down my chin. "Oops," I said.

Mullen said, "I'll take care of you later, Carey."

He said it as if it were a threat, which surprised me. In fact, I was surprising myself. I generally don't go out of my way to be offensive.

I went downstairs to find the whole group on their knees, saying the rosary. The pastor was leading them. I sat on the staircase until they finished. "Pray for us sinners, now and at the hour of our death. Amen." I wondered why the pastor had come instead of Father Frank Garvin, who was probably one of the few people on earth who had liked Tom Costigan.

We got rid of the mourners in record time, all except Cousin Agnes. "I'm staying with you, you poor dear," she said to Alice. "People shouldn't be alone at a time like this."

I was having a little trouble articulating. I said, "That's very kind of you, Cousin Agnes, but you go have some fun. I'll stay with Alice."

The woman looked at me in disbelief, then shock. "But . . . but—"

"Not to worry," I said, using the British expression of an uncle on my mother's side. "I'll take good care of her."

The woman's face took on a knowing look.

I called to Hugh Mullen, "Get a cab for Cousin Agnes, Hughie old man. She's only going to the Sheraton Centre, but we think she'd be safer if she rode."

Outside, Alice said, "We really should have walked her to the hotel."

"Could you have stood another fifteen minutes of her?" I asked. Alice made a face, and I said, "Neither could I."

We walked hand in hand on what was becoming our accustomed route—over to Ninth Avenue, then down Ninth past cross-streets to Alice's. The sky was completely overcast, and a strong, chill wind was coming from the north.

"Feels good," Alice said.

"Feels good," I agreed.

When we turned to cross the first intersection, her hand was lightly on my arm. I heard the sudden roar of an engine, the screech of tires, Alice's cry of "Eddie!" Her hand tightened, then I was off balance, plunging forward through the air. I said, "What . . . what?" Then I landed heavily on my sore shoulder, my cheek scraped on pavement, a rush of air went by behind me, and my mind was in a black swirl.

I squirmed, and said, "What . . . what?" I tried to get my hands under me to push myself away from the embrace of the pavement. One hand touched something repellently squishy and the other touched Alice. I looked at the squishy thing and saw that it was a cigar butt in a puddle. I pulled my hand away. I said, "What . . . what?"

Alice lugged me to my feet, or at least helped me; I was too big and heavy for her to do it alone. There was a sharp pain on the side of my head, and my shoulder was throbbing. I peered at Alice, saw the look of concern on her face. I also saw the blotch of blood and dirt on her elbow. I said, "Ooh," cringing in sympathy.

"Just a scrape," she said shakily. "How about you?"

"Never better," I said. I took a step toward her, stepped on something sharp, and realized I was in my stocking feet.

She said, "Look," pointing behind me. I turned, and saw my loafers in the middle of the intersection, crushed out of shape. I looked at her dumbly.

"The truck ran over them," she said.

"We were nearly run over," I said.

"Yes."

"And you saved my life."

She didn't reply, simply gazed at me with big eyes.

"You pulled me right out of my shoes," I said.

She said, "Your face—"

I shouted, "You pulled me right out of my shoes!" And I started to laugh. "Wonderful!" I said, hugging her.

She said "Eddie" several times, and I let her go.

I went to retrieve my shoes.

She said, "Leave them.",

I said, "They're new. My only pair of black loafers. I bought them for the syndicate party."

I picked them up, straightened them as best I could, and slid my feet into them. "I was just breaking them in," I said.

"They're ruined," she said.

"Better than walking barefoot." I had to shuffle to keep them from falling off. The avenue was quite deserted.

We resumed our walk home. I noticed she had a slight limp.

"Nothing to worry about," she said.

At the next intersection, I said, "What was it?"

"A panel truck. Came out of nowhere. Speeding."

"We could have been killed," I said. "And you saved me."

"Eddie," she said. "Eddie, listen. I think someone did try to kill us."

We were again walking hand in hand. It was then that I noticed that she was lugging her briefcase in her other hand. Her attachment to it was so idiotically endearing that I hugged her again.

"Did you hear what I said?"

I said, "I'm trying not to think about it."

When we came to Alice's house, many things that had been racing about loosely in my mind came together like speeding cars in a fog, and the fear that I had been fending off with whiskey and whimsy suddenly locked me in place. Two things were wrong. The street light was out, and there was no cop on the stoop.

I said, "You're not going in there."

She said, "Stop it, Eddie. Of course I am. Come on up, and we'll put something on your face."

I clung to her to keep her from going up the stoop.

"Alice, honey, darling, sweetheart... No! You're no longer under the protection of the police, and I'm not either. We're on our own, and you said it yourself, someone just tried to kill us. Look at the house—not a light in the place. We'd be going in blind. First they murdered your kitchen, then they knocked hell out of my shoes. What would they kill this time? Your briefcase? All those compositions you never get around to marking?"

She glanced at the house, then at me. "Maybe we're just imagining—"

"Maybe we are," I said, "but you're not going in there." I took her by the arm. "Come on."

"Wait, let me just shove the briefcase inside the door. It's beginning to weigh a ton." She ran up the steps, dropped her case in the vestibule, and returned to me. "I feel a hundred pounds lighter," she said.

As we limped toward my apartment, I in my crumpled loafers and she with a banged knee, my mind started rationalizing.

"I never saw the damn truck," I said.

"I did," she said.

"Are you sure it wasn't some kids joyriding?"

"Face it, Eddie. That driver deliberately tried to run us down."

"I wasn't looking where I was going."

"I was," she said.

I said, "Street lights go out all the time. The house was dark because you forgot to put on the hall light before you left. And the police just don't have the manpower to assign round-the-clock protection to people like us. And that gets us thinking—"

"It's all just a series of coincidences, is that what you're saying?"

"Not exactly, but—"

"Why don't we go back, then?" she asked. She stopped walking. We were nearly to my apartment.

"No, I was just trying to put things in perspective."

She said, "Honestly, Eddie," and she shook her head.

When we finally made it to my apartment, I went around closing and locking windows and turned the air conditioner on low.

She said, "We don't need that. It's cool outside."

"A man's home is his castle," I said. "I just pulled up the drawbridges. I always do that."

"Of course," she said. She stood in the center of the living room and looked forlornly at her dress. "I feel like I've been wallowing in the gutter," she said.

"You have," I said. "What you need is a good shower, and then we'll take a look at that elbow and knee."

"And your face," she said.

While she was in the bathroom, I scrubbed my hands in the kitchen sink, got out of my soiled clothes, put on a cotton robe, and poured myself a Scotch on the rocks. My face felt stiff, and the side of my head hurt. I carried the drink into the small room I had made into my den—I liked the idea of having a den, as if I were a cultured man with inherited wealth—and plunked down on the daybed. Rich men's dens don't have daybeds, or word processors either, for that matter, but what the hell, if I call it a den, it's a den.

I looked at the hooded Kaypro and said, "Ira."

I retrieved the floppy disk from my jacket pocket, dragged myself to the machine, and turned it on. I inserted my WordStar disk and the "IRA" disk, hoping it would give me a clue to Ira's identity. If it wasn't in WordStar, I was sunk. I hadn't the foggiest notion of how to use any of the other processes that had come with the set.

The contents of Max's disk showed on the screen: "IRA." I hit "D," typed "IRA," pressed the return button, and there it was:

```
6/12–$5000 rec'd.
6/12–$5000 to Banque Suisse #68521
6/23–$25,000 rec'd.
6/23–$25,000 to Banque Suisse #68521
7/12–$20,000 rec'd.
7/13–$20,000 to Banque Suisse #68521
```

* * *

I pressed "C" to roll the copy upward, and the blinking words on the screen said: WARM BOOT.

Shit, I thought with a groan, something was wrong with the disk. I never did find out what to do when the damned computer started shouting "warm boot" at me. My solution was to go back and start over, which I did. But when I got to the same point on the disk, the damn screen flashed the same two idiotic words.

"Warm boot! Warm boot!" I snarled at it. "You're the dumbest damn machine I ever saw!"

Alice stood in the doorway. "A man's in a sorry state when he talks back to a computer," she said.

"Nuts," I said. "I must have ruined Max's disk when I slid into second." I flicked the machine off and stretched, causing the shoulder wound to hurt. "Ooh," I said.

She said, "Come on, Eddie, it's your turn." She was in my terrycloth beach robe, a shortie that reached to mid-thigh. The long, slim legs fascinated me.

"How . . . how's the knee?" I managed to say.

"A slight swelling. Nothing to worry about," she said.

"Let me see," I said, reaching out to touch it.

She intercepted my arm and said, "Never mind about my knee. We're going to wash your face and see what's underneath." She started to march me to the bathroom.

"Okay, okay," I cried. "I can do it myself."

I took one look at my face in the mirror and decided to take a shower. The dirt was not only on my scraped cheek, but matted in my whiskers as well. The hot water stung like crazy, and drove thoughts of long slim legs out of my mind.

Afterward, while I stood there like an overgrown child with a bath towel around my middle, Alice dabbed some Unguentine on the raw spots and changed the dressing on my shoulder.

Then I dug out an old Ace bandage and insisted on wrapping it around her twisted knee. I was panting when I finished. Alice tried to preserve her modesty, but the short robe kept foiling her, just as my treacherous bath towel failed to hide my own arousal.

We faced each other in the bathroom.

"What a couple of sad sacks we are," I said, and I embraced her.

She clutched me tightly, her mouth on mine, her hands on my bare back. I became aware that my bath towel was on the floor, and my hands were caressing—wonder of wonders—bare flesh! Amazing! We stood breast to breast and thigh to thigh. She lowered her arms, and the robe slipped away completely. I felt a pulsing in my abdomen, and I didn't know whether it was her heartbeat or mine, or whether there was now but one heartbeat and one bloodstream for the two of us.

Much later, I lay on the daybed and stared at the ceiling. I had had no trouble getting to sleep when we had at last said our good nights, but two hours later, I woke up with the need to go to the bathroom. Back in bed, I was wide awake. My wounds ached, my head hurt, my innards were in an uproar. I felt wretchedly powerless. Somehow, without knowing how, I had a wildcat by the tail, with no way of letting go, and the beast was out to claw Alice as well as me.

Alice in the next room. Her long, slender body in my bed! The facade of her cool intelligence breached by an uprush of sensuality. And though I had botched our embrace, I knew that we fit together the way God intended in the Garden of Eden—without hindrance.

Hey, Max, if you're listening, I think I'm going to make it, never mind my gosh-awful performance! I'm a little late, by most people's standards—hell, Alice and I are going through what you and everybody else went through at sixteen—but not too late. I know it's not too late. It's never too late. . . . Is it?

Max materialized in my mind's eye as he was at the syndicate party, dancing with the most beautiful woman in the room. Then he was watching her dance with somebody else. Son of a gun, it was Tom Costigan she was dancing with, and he was saying proudly, "Ain't she something!" Proud, and yet I sensed his uneasiness. Bewitched, bothered, and bewildered. He was someone under a spell, and I felt a deep sadness for him.

She wasn't worth it, Max, that was what I was trying to say to you but couldn't. Honor O'Toole is Irish trash, but I guess she got you in your blind spot.

Dishonor O'Toole.

My computer screen flashed in my mind: "Honor of IRA." And suddenly I groaned. I knew with a terrible clarity what the witch of Hell's Kitchen had been doing to the sweetest man I had ever known.

Abel, beloved son of Adam and Eve, was slain again. Not by Cain, his brother, but by Honor, his temptress.

Oh, shit, Max.

11

"The Irish Republican Army!" Alice exclaimed. "Glory be!"

She sat across from me at my small kitchen table, looking to me like the most beautiful woman in the world. She was more sedately garbed in my cotton robe this morning, while her dress was drying on a hanger in the bathroom. We pretended not to notice that our knees were touching under the table, concentrating instead on our breakfast of scrambled eggs, toast, and coffee. It was close to eight o'clock, but neither of us was in a rush to get to work, so we took delight in dawdling over the meal. She had been given leave from school because of her father's death.

"Maybe I'm wrong," I said slowly. "It's only a guess, nothing the police could take to the DA, but all the little pieces seem to fit."

Alice said, "Up the revolution! I didn't think there was a patriotic bone in that woman's overripe body."

"Is that what the IRA is?" I asked. "A group of patriots?"

"Certainly. Don't you think so? All they want to do is

unite their country, and the British are playing dog-in-the-manger. Of course, I don't justify all their tactics—"

"Alice honey," I said. "These people are murderers, pure and simple. They're terrorists, and they don't care who gets slaughtered, so long as—"

"Oh, you're talking about a small minority," she said. "The Provisional Wing, I believe they're called. They're like the Mau Mau in Kenya—"

"I don't care about the Mau Mau in Kenya—"

"They were called Kikuyu, the Mau Mau. Kikuyu, meaning, 'Get out! Get out!' They were saying it to the British, and that's what the Provos are saying in Ireland. 'Get out! Get out!'"

I broke off the knee contact and stared down at my plate.

"Eddie," she said.

I raised my eyes. "Are you finished with the Mau Mau?"

"If you say so, Eddie."

"I was trying to explain my brilliant series of deductions, and all you can say is, 'Get out! Get out!'"

"Yes, Eddie," she said with suspicious meekness.

"I was talking about the disk I took from Max's apartment," I said, knowing that I sounded sulky. "I first thought IRA might be a man, Ira. Then, when I saw the entries showing deposits of money, I thought it might be one of those Individual Retirement Accounts, either his or someone else's. Then, in the middle of the night, I remembered that the heading on the disk said not just 'IRA' but 'HONOR OF IRA,' and my mind went *click*."

"Click?"

"Aren't you interested in finding out who tried to kill us last night?"

"I refuse to believe it was the IRA."

I shoved my eggs away unfinished. "Bear with me," I said. "You can look on it as an Irish fairy tale if you like, a bedtime story containing three murders and the attempted murders of you and me, dear heart. Ready?"

She nodded.

"Once upon a time," I said, "some snotty college kids in the Midwest built themselves a toy atom bomb. One of them is an Arab patriot... this story is filled with patriots. So this Arab patriot snatches the toy bomb and gives it to other Arab patriots here in New York. But before the poor Arabs can put it to constructive use in Beirut or possibly Washington, D.C., along comes this patriotic Irish-American gunsel, who happens to be a thief by trade, and he accidentally steals the toy bomb and he sells it for thirty pieces of silver. Are you with me so far?"

Alice barely nodded.

"Okay," I continued. "Unfortunately, the thief discovers he has a conscience, and instead of going out and doing the correct thing, namely, hanging himself, he involves other people. Being a patriotic thief, he goes to the one man, another Irish-American, who he thinks can save the U.S. and the world from disaster. He tells the whole story to Tom Costigan and probably gives him something that will bear out the story or in some way pin down the people who bought the bomb. So far, we don't know who those people are, do we?"

"Not yet. But we know, don't we, that they must be people who are sympathetic to the IRA, right?"

I sighed. "Yes, I think so. May I go on?"

"Please."

"Okay. The thief told someone else. He went to confession. To an Irish-American priest. He probably picked on Frank Garvin, figuring that Garvin was a rumdum and would immediately forget what he had been told in the confessional. But poor Frank not only didn't forget, he became haunted by what he had heard, and he wound up spilling it to me."

I took a sip of coffee and grimaced. "I know I'm leaving out bits and pieces; my mind keeps going blank on me. Anyway, let's assume, just to give the bad guys a name, that it's the IRA that got the bomb from Danny Dunn. I deduce that the IRA doesn't know about Dunn's confession to Frank, because Frank is still living—at least, he is as far as I know. But the other two people are dead—murdered—your father blown to bits and Dunn with his throat cut. Obvious killings. But these people can't pile killing on killing without having them connected by the police. So the next killing has to be made to look like something else, a suicide."

Alice frowned. "You're saying that Max Abel was murdered."

"I'm certain of it," I said.

"Why?"

"He was laundering money for the IRA," I said. "And he was about to tell about it. He was going to blow the whistle."

"Why would a man like Max Abel do such a criminally foolish thing as to—"

"For love," I said. "Call it infatuation rather than love. He was a homely little guy in his sixties with waning powers. Then along comes this luscious piece of Irish-American ass who tells him that he's still the greatest lover in creation. God only knows what she told him to justify the laundering, but—"

"I saw them at the party," Alice said. "She had him twisted around her little finger. But how are you so sure he was washing their money?"

I let my shoulders slump. "I'm not sure. But it's a fact that he was transferring money to a Swiss account for Honor of IRA. And he was doing it, damn it, for the bitch who was screwing him deaf, dumb, and blind. But the funds weren't hers; they belonged to the IRA. How else can you interpret it?"

"And that's the only connection to the IRA? The heading on the computer disk?"

"The only specific one. But you have to remember the phony-baloney poet who's her regular consort. And the recent doings in Belfast. And the fear that was in Frank Garvin. If Danny Dunn had passed the bomb on to, say, Iranian terrorists or to some other terrorist group, I don't think Father Frank would have taken it quite so hard.

But Irish terrorists—that was bringing it closer to home, at least to an Irish-American with ties to the old sod."

"It's pretty thin," Alice said. "And how do you know Max was going to blow the whistle? Did he say he was going to the police? What did he say?"

"God, Alice, maybe I should have been a priest, after all," I said. "Everybody seems to want to go to confession to me. Max said he had something important to tell me about one of the contributors. I think he had made up his mind to cut off his connection with the IRA, let Honor be damned. But he liked me and didn't want me or the syndicate to be hurt. The only guess I can come up with is that one of the contributors is a member of this IRA outfit. I don't know, maybe I'm imagining things, but I can't help thinking that the reason he was killed was that he was going to tell me something that would be harmful to the group. He definitely said it was about one of the contributors."

"He didn't say who."

"No."

"Pretty thin."

"Thin as the emperor's clothes."

"I can't believe the IRA would use an atom bomb. My God, there would be no controlling the death and destruction—"

"The madmen in it would."

She shook her head. "My father was always sympathetic to the cause. And to think that—" She held up her hand. "Wait. They were looking for something. It's possible, it's just possible I have it. Listen. The night after they dropped the grenade—no, it was the next night—my father came up. I was busy, I don't know what I was doing, and he said, 'Don't be surprised if you come across something of mine in here. Just leave it there, all right, Princess?'"

"Princess?"

"He occasionally called me that. I wasn't paying much attention, but I think he was holding my briefcase."

"He put something in your briefcase?"

"I don't know."

"Interesting," I said. "Now the question is, which of the contributors could be mixed up with the IRA? It would have to be an Irishman... I mean someone of Irish extraction, wouldn't you think?"

Alice stood up. "I'm going right over and have a look," she said.

I said, "The trouble is, I have no idea who's Irish and who isn't. Rocky Caputo, the puzzle editor, you wouldn't take him for an Irishman, would you? But he's as Irish as I am. He once told me his mother was Irish. It was a Saint Patrick's Day, and we were kidding around—" I saw that Alice wasn't there, so I stopped talking.

I mentally went down the list of contributors, and was surprised at how lost I was in picking out Irish names. Is White an Irish name? Is Smith? I didn't know. The only out-and-out Irisher I could think of was the lace-curtain bastard, J. P. Cosgrove.

I called out to Alice, "Can you picture J. P. Cosgrove as a bog-trotting revolutionary?"

She didn't answer, but I laughed at the thought.

I said, "Did you ever think of Glass as an Irish name?"

This time she answered. "Who?"

"David Glass."

"What about him?" she asked, coming into the room, now dressed.

"Would he be Irish?"

"Anyone with any sense would like to be," she said. "But he's too peculiar. I'd vote against admitting him."

"Thanks," I said.

She said, "I'm going back to the house."

I stood up. "And I'm going to have a word with Father Frank Garvin. I'll meet you at the house in an hour."

I took her in my arms. "Be extra careful," I said. "You're probably safer in the daytime, but... be careful."

"You, too," she said.

Our lips met, and I foggily remembered a line of poetry about "coffee-scented kisses." The title of the poem was "This Is My Beloved." I couldn't dredge up the poet's name. But so be it, I thought, holding her tightly. This is my beloved.

The fat woman who opened the rectory door said that Father Frank Garvin wasn't there. I asked when he was due back, and she said, "Nivver, sir. He's been transferred."

"To another parish?"

"I'm not permitted to say." Her eyes were trying to tell me something, which I didn't get.

Instead, I got the pastor. He was a short, powerful-looking man, with salt stains at the armpits of his cassock. He glared at me through puffy eyes.

"You've done your damage, Mr. Carey. Now what do you want?"

Bewildered, I said, "Just to talk to Frank, that's all. Your housekeeper said—"

"That the poor man's been transferred," the pastor said. "It's true. He's beyond your reach, and I want you to stay away from his replacement, or I personally will beat you to a pulp. Do you hear, Mr. Carey?"

"What'd I do, Father? What'd I do?"

The pastor's small eyes blazed. "Did you think I didn't know what was going on? You and people like you feeding alcohol to the poor, weak soul! He's in a sanitarium, Mr. Carey, and only God knows if he'll ever be able to exercise his priestly duties again. I hope you feel proud of yourself."

"What . . . what happened?"

"I've told you enough," the pastor said. "Pray to God for forgiveness."

He closed the big door, nearly squashing my fingers in the process.

I stood there for several minutes, unable to move. Then I looked up at the sky. The massive clouds frowned down at me, and a strong wind, coming down the street from the east, was tossing my hair and whiskers every which way.

"Damn it, damn it, damn it," I muttered. "I've never felt this low in my whole life."

I left the rectory steps and charged east into the wind, feeling that if I stopped to brood I would come dangerously close to killing myself.

The gusts were surprisingly fierce, and if I had spotted a free cab, I would have succumbed and hailed it. Naturally, the few cabs I saw were either occupied or off duty. I fought my way crosstown and up to the Sixties. I was on a fool's errand, but it was an errand that had to be done. Some questions had to be put to the eminent author J. P. Cosgrove, and there was no way I could get the police to do it.

"Lieutenant," I would say to Ferrante, "I believe that J. P. Cosgrove is behind these murders."

"Oh," Ferrante would say. "What makes you say that?"

"He's the only Irish contributor to the syndicate."

"Okay, Carey, I'll go right up there and give him the third degree."

Sure, sure.

The trouble was, I would speak to Cosgrove, he would be insulted and holler to Hawthorne, our idiot publisher, and I would get canned from probably the only job I had any talent to fill. I would be out of work, I would drink heavily, and wind up on the Bowery or as a male bag woman on the subway.

The wind blew grit in my eyes, and I felt very sorry for myself.

What did I know about Cosgrove? I had written the biographical release for the column's promotion kit. Okay, he was born and raised in the Boston area, scion to a family in comfortable circumstances, rather like the Fitzgeralds and the Kennedys. That's what the release said. He was at one time married to the daughter of an old New England family, and she drank herself to death.

The release didn't say that, but I inferred it from the early date of her death and from the sort of man Cosgrove was. Not much else was known of his life before his first book, *The Bastards of Boston*, became a best-seller.

What could I ask him?

"Was your first book about the Cosgrove family?"

Whammo, out of a job.

His street was only a few blocks from Max Abel's. The surviving town houses on it had clean facades—all except one. Cosgrove's was grimy—"the patina of age," he called it—and covered with English ivy, which had bugs but also its own cachet of old money.

Without pausing, I mounted his front stoop and jabbed his doorbell. If I had paused to reflect, I would have turned around and gone back home. That damned question—"Was your first book about the Cosgrove family?"—kept going through my mind, and I was afraid I would blurt it out.

His man Stanhope opened the door. He was a tall, balding man built on the order of Arthur Treacher, and I imagined him learning the art of being a butler from watching Treacher movies. Snooty.

He admitted me to the front hall and said, "I'm afraid you've come at a poor time. We were just getting ready to leave for the cottage. Perhaps another time?"

I resisted an impulse to bust him in the chops, not only because I was a civilized man but because he looked powerful enough to whomp me back and kick my butt.

I said, "Tell Mr. Cosgrove I only want a minute of his time."

Stanhope went up the staircase, leaving me—rather rudely, I thought—in the dimly lit hall. I looked about me, caught sight of myself in a mirror, and almost forgave Stanhope his rudeness. I looked more than ever like a wild man.

The polished table beneath the mirror had a small stack of mail. Atop the mail was an unfolded sheet of paper, which had obviously come out of an envelope. I moved closer and looked without touching, and a shock wave zitted through my body. What I saw was a poem.

COSTIGAN'S WAKE
Blue-jawed, wild-eyed, felon-fanged
Beast unleashed, chortling with English glee . . .

The sound of Cosgrove's highfalutin voice made me jump back. "Yes, Mr. Carey?" it said. The great author stood at the head of the stairs, seeming to fill it like a lumpy, wingless Nike of Samothrace.

"May I have a minute, J. P.?" I said, tentatively moving toward the stairs. This was going to be an awkward conversation if it was to be conducted up the length of the staircase.

"Speak, man," he commanded me.

"Well," I said. "It's about Max Abel." I started to climb the stairs.

"I scarcely knew the man," he said impatiently. "I believe I met him for the first time at your disastrous party."

I inched farther up the stairs.

"That may be true, sir," I said. "But he told me—I'm only saying what he said—he told me that you were a secret member of the IRA, and it's important to me to find out—"

The fruity voice interrupted me. "I'm not a joiner, Mr. Carey. You should know that. Now, whatever this IRA is—"

"The Irish Republican Army."

"The answer to your question is no. The Irish Republican Army, indeed! I find your question offensive. If that's all, Stanhope will show you out."

"I'm glad to hear your answer," I said. "I'm truly relieved. You see, this small group of patriots has gotten hold of an atom bomb, and I thought you ought to know—"

"You're a blithering idiot, Carey," he said.

"You're right, sir," I blithered. "You're absolutely right. I shouldn't have come here with a wild story like that."

He raised his hand as if to give me absolution or stop traffic. "Since you *are* here, perhaps you can make yourself useful." He turned to Stanhope, who had remained in the background. "The column is in the study." The butler retreated.

Cosgrove turned to me. "I was about to call the messenger service, but you can do it just as well. Take the column back to Mr. Godbold."

I was still a few steps below him. "Er . . . I wasn't going back."

"I think you had best take it, Mr. Carey," he said. "That is, if you think you're capable of doing it."

"Oh, I can do it," I assured him.

He remained motionless, his eyes fixed somewhere in the gloom over my head.

I laughed. "Funny how I misunderstood Max Abel. Obviously, he said some other name, and I heard him wrong."

His gaze flicked down to me for a freeze-dried instant, and he turned away.

I said, "It's just that I don't understand how Irish-Americans can support the terrorism—"

"There are many things you don't understand, Edward," he said, "including Shakespeare's adage, 'Fools rush in where angels fear to tread.'"

"Er . . . I don't think it was Shakespeare—"

"Ah, here's the column," the great man said. He took the folded sheets from Stanhope and passed them down to me. "To Godbold and no one else. You understand that?"

My sense of outrage erupted through the damper I had put on it. I stood mute.

He said to the butler, "Give him ten dollars. That's the messenger-service fee, isn't it?"

I turned and went down the stairs.

At the bottom, I looked back up at him. I said, "Tell

Brendan Power there's no such thing as 'English glee.' They have every emotion but glee. That's their tragedy."

He made no reply.

I went to the front door, shrugged, and said to myself: *What the hell.* I turned and said loudly, "One other question, Mr. Cosgrove. Was your first book about the Cosgrove family in Boston?"

I opened the door and went out into the blustery rain. Despite having just tossed away the job I loved, I felt elated. I turned my face into the rain and smiled broadly.

My half-English, half-Irish glee didn't last long. I had just confirmed to the IRA, if they needed confirmation, that I was on their trail, stumbling and thrashing about and grasping at inconsequential threads though I was, and that they were correct in trying to put me out of business. I had let the Bastard of Boston know that I had discovered the connection between him and the Hibernian Bard of Balderdash, and their elation over the murder of Tom Costigan.

And I still had nothing I could take to Lieutenant Ferrante. Everything I knew so far was, in the language of lawyers, irrelevant, incompetent, and immaterial.

Worse still, I had probably confirmed the IRA's suspicions of Alice. What I knew she must know, too. I had to get back to Alice right away.

The wind at my back propelled me toward Hell's Kitchen. On Fifty-seventh Street, I passed an entranceway I knew. I fought my way back to it. Yes, on one of the upper floors was the studio apartment of David Glass. On the questionable theory that assassins were daunted by rainstorms and remained holed up until the storm had passed lest they get wet, I put off returning to Alice's for a few minutes and entered the doorway to David's building. I discovered that the tan windbreaker I had donned when I left home was not waterproof. I was soaked through, and starting to shiver.

The building was an ancient one not yet replaced by modern glitz, an office building in which it was technically illegal for Glass to have living quarters. But this was his home as well as his studio. I rode up in a whining elevator, got off at the fifth floor, and squished down the drab hallway. The nameplate on his door had two names: David Glass and Mario Baldi.

When he opened the door, he gaped at me in surprise.

"I have an appointment with Mayor Baldi," I said, and moved past him into the large room.

"Father Carey," he said uncertainly. "Come in." His tall, taut body was dressed in a white shirt, dark slacks, and sheepskin slippers. His dark hair was tousled, and a look of some dark passion was fading from his handsome face to be replaced by blankness.

The room itself was schizophrenic. I had been here before, but the division of the two halves had never seemed so distinct. On the one side was his slanted drawing board, comic cartoons pinned haphazardly to a cork wall. The other side appeared to be the aftermath of an explosion in a ketchup factory. Here was an artist's easel, and a bank of oil paintings, expertly framed, pretty much covered the whole wall. The paintings were wildly abstract, all with glistening blood-red as the dominant color.

I said, "I'm on messenger duty this morning. I picked up Cosgrove's column, and as I was passing here said to myself, I wonder if David has a batch ready for delivery."

He said, "They're not due until Wednesday, Father." He said it sullenly.

I put on my disarming grin. "I know," I said. "Actually, I didn't come here for that. I was caught in the rain, and I was hoping you had a cup of hot coffee for a poor wayfarin' stranger."

"Sure," he said, moving to his kitchenette. "Sit down. The water's still hot."

I sat on his threadbare sofa in the middle of the room, then rebounded to my feet. "I'm wet," I said. I moved about the room restlessly. I stopped at the painting on the easel. "What are you working on, David?" The painting appeared to be a cascade of blood. On the stand beside the easel was an unfolded sheet of paper. I picked it up.

The young cartoonist came to me swiftly and snatched the sheet from my hands. "That wouldn't interest you, Father," he said.

All I had a chance to see was the title at the top: "Costigan's Wake."

"Just black," I said. "No sugar."

I went to the window and looked out at the rear of another building. "Great view," I said. "Looks like the rain is letting up."

"It's the edge of the hurricane," David said, handing me a steaming mug.

"Ah," I said, wrapping my hands around it.

"Radio said it's sideswiping us and heading out into the ocean." He gestured toward the sofa. "Sit down for a minute, Father. I'm sorry you can't stay long. I was just getting ready to go out."

I sat on the edge of the sofa. He sat opposite me in a straight-back wooden chair.

I said, "Hurricanes are the real revolutions."

After a moment, he said, "How's that?"

"It's a dumb theory of mine," I said. I sipped some of the hot liquid before I spoke again. "High-pressure areas revolve clockwise, and low-pressure areas go counterclockwise."

He looked puzzled. "Yeah?"

I said, "Hurricanes are the deepest and strongest of the low-pressure areas. They are counterrevolutions. They bring violence and destruction."

"Oh," he said.

"Which are you, David?" I asked. "Some people are revolutionaries, but they bring on the counterrevolutions, which are much more violent and leave many deaths in their wakes. It's my theory that people who throw bombs are not revolutionaries at all, but counterrevolutionaries."

He nodded. "That's interesting," he said.

"Which are you, David?" I asked again.

He squirmed slightly. "Neither, Father," he said. "I'm just a poor cartoonist trying to make people laugh."

"By showing Mayor Baldi blowing up Tom Costigan?"

He stood up. "Oh, crap, Father," he said. "Are you on that thing again?"

I made a soothing gesture. "Sit down, David," I said. "I'm simply interested in the connection between violence and humor. When Bugs Bunny or the Roadrunner blows up the wolf who's chasing him, that's funny. But when the IRA blows up an innocent shopper in Harrod's in the heart of London, can that ever be funny? Or is it an act of murder?"

"You don't understand," he said, unconsciously parroting Cosgrove. His voice had a harsh rasp to it. "You're confusing things. I don't know how the IRA got into this, but the IRA is at war, and that's a damn lot different from Bugs Bunny splattering the Big Bad Wolf. A whole damn lot different!"

I peered at him over my mug of coffee. "Are you saying that all's fair in love and war?"

"I'm not saying anything. You're the one who's doing all the saying."

"You're right, of course," I said. "You have to forgive me. I've been involved in three murders in three days. I suppose the IRA would consider them executions or, to use your expression, three war casualties. Anyway, I'm a bit shook up. And I keep asking myself, when is violence justified? That's why I became fixated on Mayor Baldi. Forgive me."

"It's okay," he said.

"I mean, take Mort Laser. He had Rube accidentally blow up the outhouse, with Pappy inside. That was funny because, although Pappy was blown sky-high, his only complaint was the Sears Roebuck catalog was ruined. Do you see the difference?"

"You don't understand," he said again. "Seaport City is at war with Portsea. *At war!* When a country is at war and it finds a spy, what does it do? It kills him. Mayor Baldi was killing a spy, that's all, and you're making a federal case of it."

I said, "But the spy was Tom Costigan, wasn't he?"

"No!" he shouted. "You're saying that, not me!" He moved about in great agitation. "Look, I'm Mayor Baldi. My city is at war. I'm armed." He looked around, snatched up a machete that I hadn't noticed from the stand beside the easel. He brandished it. "I'm armed, and that—that chair—is the enemy. What do I do? Do I blow him up and say, Sorry about your Sears Roebuck catalog? No, I smash him!"

Gripping the weapon with two hands, he brought it down on the back of the wooden chair, splitting it in two.

"He's not dead yet!" he cried, and the blade came down on the chair seat and through the rungs below. Even as the chair was falling apart, he swung again and again.

I said, "It's dead, David."

He stood over it, panting.

Suddenly, he laughed. "Now, that's funny," he said. "If you don't think it's funny, you don't know what funny is."

I said, "You killed an innocent chair."

"That's what you think," he said more calmly. "I got it at the Salvation Army. Paid two dollars for it. I was going to get rid of it anyway. Good riddance, chair."

I stood up, handed him my cup. "I've got to run, David. Thanks for the coffee. You saved my life."

He stood there with the machete in one hand and the cup in the other. "Any time," he said apathetically.

He didn't move while I went out the door and closed it.

I didn't wait for the elevator; I clumped down the iron staircase and out onto the sidewalk. The rain had eased up, but the wind was now coming from the northeast, its velocity intensified. A real nor'easter, by cracky, I told myself. I let it propel me across Fifty-seventh Street and down Eighth Avenue. The sidewalks, which were generally thronged at noon on a Monday, were almost deserted.

I'm in a bad dream, I told myself. The cars seemed to

move silently. The only sound was the rush of wind and the creaking of signs swinging in the gusts. Everyone had gone insane. Did David Glass really butcher a chair with a machete? Did everyone in the goddamn city get a copy of Brendan Power's snickering verse? Or have I gone bonkers? Am I just imagining that fright, rather than the wind, is propelling me to Alice's house? I felt the shove of the air and the knot of pain in my stomach, and decided it was both.

Mullen's Funeral Parlor came first. On the chance that Alice had gone there, I rushed in. The smell of flowers sickened me. Tom Costigan was alone in his final sleep. "Hey, Tom," I greeted him, and headed for the stairs.

Hugh Mullen was coming down. "What the hell are you doing here?" he greeted me.

In response to my question, he said that Alice wasn't there, and that he didn't expect her until evening.

I turned to leave.

"Too bad about Father Frank," he said.

I paused.

"It was bound to happen sooner or later," Mullen said. "The poor devil could sure put away the sauce. Imagine, a whole bottle of Jameson!"

"What's that about Jameson?" I asked.

"Didn't you know? He passed out in the alley beside the rectory holding a fifth of Irish whiskey. Empty. That could kill a man, do you know that?"

"When was this?"

"Saturday night. When the pastor called me, I was glad to arrange transportation." He had a pious smirk on his face.

"Are you sure it was Jameson?"

"I saw the bottle," he said. "Incidentally, you'll be getting a bill in the mail for the cabinet."

I stumbled out into the storm. Now I knew I was crazy. Or someone was. Father Frank Garvin would drink anything alcoholic *except* Irish whiskey. "Tastes like iron filings," he had once told me, apologizing for rejecting a product of Ireland.

I hastened to Alice's with the awful knowledge that the IRA had spirited away the fourth person who knew of their conspiracy. That left only Alice and myself to be dealt with. *Dear God, I shouldn't have let her out of my sight.*

I started to run.

12

Alice's faraway voice said, "Who is it?"

My body slumped in relief. I said loudly into the intercom, "It's me."

"Eddie?"

"You were expecting maybe President Reagan?"

The door latch hummed. I shoved the door open and headed up the stairs on the run, seeing in my imagination the hatchway to the roof open and a man descending, a machete gripped in his teeth the way pirates did in old-time movies. I halted on the top landing, peered up the dark well, climbed up three rungs, and saw that the padlock was in place.

Alice, perched on the sofa, was gazing at me in astonishment through the open doorway. Some papers were spread out on the coffee table before her.

"You look like a wild man," she said.

I stepped down from the ladder and entered. "Tell me something I don't know."

She said, "Come take a look at this." Excitement glowed in her face.

I lowered myself in the chair opposite her, my eyes

fixed on the papers. Some were typed, some were handwritten in pencil, some were white bond, others were lined pages from a yellow legal-size pad.

"My father's notes," she said breathlessly. "You won't believe this. I can't believe it myself. You were right about the great author. How did you ever—"

Her gaze swiveled upward over my head. "Eddie! Behind you!"

I started to rise and turn. Then my head exploded.

Alice was in danger, but somehow she didn't know it. She was marching in a parade, proudly walking with that long fluid gait of hers that made me recall lines of poetry from my high school days: "Whenas in silks my Julia goes / Then, then (methinks) how sweetly flows / That liquefaction of her clothes." She was in the pale-blue dress that I loved so dearly, but she was marching with a platoon of nuns in wimples and robes. I heard the skirl of bagpipes and the beat of drums. Could it be St. Patrick's Day? I didn't recognize the street, a mean street something like Ninth Avenue. The spectators lining the street were all dressed in green and smoked white clay pipes. They looked like smiling billygoats.

I ran along the sidewalk calling to Alice, but she didn't hear me. My loafers didn't fit, and I kept stumbling. A panel truck raced out of a side street and bore down on the group of nuns, who all nimbly leaped out of the way, leaving only Alice in its path. I knew the truck contained an atomic explosive. The spectators were applauding, and howling in glee, "Liquefy her!" The truck started to expand and turn into a gigantic mushroom....

I was lying in the gutter. No, it was a carpeted floor. I opened my eyes, and was looking at the strange geometric symmetry of a skylight. The noise I heard was the rattling of the skylight in what appeared to be fierce gusts of wind. The skylight was going in and out of focus. I tried to sit up, but dizziness forced me back down. I groaned, and called to Alice. Only the skylight answered.

I sat up, and had to rest my head on my knees until the sickening dizziness subsided. "Alice!" I cried, but I knew she wasn't there.

When I was able to peer around, I saw that the coffee table was out of place; otherwise, the room was in order. I put my hand on the back of my head, felt the swelling, looked at my hand. No blood. I recalled my mother once calling my father a "thick-headed Mick." I don't think she meant it literally, but I grimly congratulated myself for taking after my father. In my haste to run up the stairs, I had probably left the front door ajar. I groaned. Another word for me—numbskull.

Alice was gone. So were her father's papers.

I made it to the telephone and, after a frustrating wait, got through to Lieutenant Ferrante. The phone line crackled.

I said, "They took her. They cracked me on the head and they took her." My throat tightened, making my hyperventilation more severe.

"Who's this? Carey? Who took who?"

"Alice Costigan," I said between gasps. "They're going... to kill her... I know it. And it's all... my fault."

He said, "Take a deep breath and hold it."

"But, damn it, Lieutenant—"

"Do it," he ordered. "Now. Deep breath."

I took a deep breath and felt myself fainting. I let it out and took another. The spasms in my diaphragm quieted.

"There," the lieutenant said. "Now, start at the beginning."

I said, "You're going to think I'm crazy, because the only real evidence I have is a bump on the back of my head and part of a floppy disk."

The story I told him was disjointed, and he had to interrupt me many times with questions. At one point, he said, "Pretty thin," and I snarled, "That's what Alice said, and now she's gone."

When I finished talking, Ferrante said, "Wait there. I'm coming right over."

"I can't," I said. "There's no time. They've got Alice."

He said, "Wait, damn it!"

I said, "I'll leave the door unlocked." And I hung up.

Suddenly, I had to sit down because my legs had no strength. I took a deep breath and held it for a long time before I let it out. Alice had said, "You were right about the great author." The fact that she said it and the way she said it made me conclude that the eminent J. P. Cosgrove was the brains of this particular group of Irish outlaws. Some brains! I didn't believe he was the one who actually zapped me and took Alice, but I felt sure it was done on his orders, and that if he didn't have Alice by this time, he certainly knew who did.

That was all I had to go on. Of all those I suspected of being members—Cosgrove, David Glass, Honor O'Toole, Brendan Power—Cosgrove was the only confirmed by Tom Costigan's notes before my lights went out.

And Cosgrove was no longer in the city. He was heading for "the cottage," Stanhope had said. I dialed Cosgrove's number, just to be sure, and got a recorded message saying he was out of town. Then I dialed David Glass's number, let it ring fifteen times, and hung up. The police can take care of Glass and the others, I thought—I didn't even know where they lived—but Cosgrove is my baby.

I knew where the cottage was. I had been there on two occasions, once with Chuck Godbold and once to get Cosgrove's okay on the brochure I wrote. The "cottage" was a Cape Cod on Dune Road in Westhampton Beach on Long Island, a deceptively modest structure on the bay side of the road, complete with a dock and boathouse for his deep-sea cruiser.

The telephone rang, but I didn't answer it. In all likelihood, I was going on a wild-goose chase, but if I let Ferrante persuade me to wait, I would be a quivering wreck, of no use to anyone. I got to my feet, swayed momentarily, and went down the stairs carefully and out into the drenching nor'easter. The chill rain seemed to clear my head.

They say you can tell the character of a man by the car he drives. Baloney. The only thing you can tell is the state of his wealth. I don't know what car I would own if I had unlimited dough. Possibly a Ferrari. But given my resources, I had settled for a Ford Escort, a nifty little car with great mileage. I garaged it by the month in an open lot near Eleventh Avenue, all I could afford. I apologized to it every time I entered it for the ravages done to it by the elements. "Sorry, old sport." And it never sulked, always started pronto, eager to go.

Driving crosstown on Forty-second Street, I had a foretaste of what awaited me on the open highway: the wipers barely able to cope with the heavy rain, the gusts of wind pushing me sideways so that I had to continually compensate by steering into it. The Midtown Tunnel was an eerie respite from the buffeting, but then I was driving into the eyeteeth of the storm. Lonely, unreal, frightening. Son of a gun, I thought, we weren't being sideswiped by the damned hurricane, we were being hit by it, head on!

I turned on the radio, 1010 WINS, the news station. The man from Accu-Weather was saying: "Hurricane Colleen is now located fifty miles due south of Jones Beach heading in a northeasterly direction toward the end of Long Island. Winds at the center are estimated at a 125 knots. Residents of the south shore of the Island, particularly those on Fire Island and the beach areas from there to Montauk, are being urged to seek higher ground. Even if the storm veers off to sea, as the weather bureau predicts that it will, the high tide and pounding surf will be enough to cause millions of dollars of damage and endanger the lives of anyone in the low-lying areas."

The regular newscaster came on to give further details of the damage already being done in the Rockaways and the Long Beach area.

I had to concentrate on driving. It was a surreal experience except for the constant fight to keep from being blown off the road. Other vehicles were moving on the Expressway, but not many, and slowly. The wind was hitting gale force only in gusts, while the rain, a greater hazard, not only cut down on visibility but collected at each side of the highway and in low areas where the drains were inadequate to handle the runoff. I tried to hold the car in the middle lane, passing cars that had stalled and others whose drivers had pulled over to wait out the deluge.

A ninety-mile drive lay ahead of me. Two hours to plan my moves. I turned the radio to a rock-and-roll station, figuring the blare of it would keep me awake.

My plan. First, I would get the screwdriver from the glove compartment and the tire iron from the trunk, and, thus armed, I would burst into Cosgrove's cottage and confront the horse-faced old bastard and his man Stanhope. Then what? "I've come for Alice." If they tried to stop me, I would smash them on the head with the iron. I would try not to kill them, but if I happened to strike them too hard, it would be no great loss to mankind, and it would save the *Herald-Courier* syndicate a large amount of money. Alice would embrace me tearfully, and we would get in the car and drive back to the city. The TV reporters would come around wanting to interview me, and I would say, "I was only fighting for the woman I love." No, I would dodge them out of modesty, and after a while they would forget about me. But Chuck Godbold would grip my hand and say, "Thanks, old buddy, you saved the syndicate." And Alice and I would get married. Where? Not in St. James the Less, but somewhere without fuss. And we would find a house in the suburbs . . .

The car was hurling me around like a big floppy beanbag, and I was gripping the steering wheel to keep from getting another concussion. My eyes came back into focus: I was on the rough grass heading for a stand of trees. I swerved back toward the highway, and the rear wheels spun in the mud. In my panic, I jammed the accelerator to the floor, fishtailing wildly. *Shit, I'm gonna get bogged down,* I thought; *the wheels are digging themselves into the earth. I'm out to save the woman I love, and I'm sinking into the ground fifty miles from nowhere!*

I prayed, *Holy Mother of God, give me a boost,* and suddenly the wind that had driven me off the road came to a breathless standstill and the wheels found traction on the shoulder. I shot back onto the highway and almost off the other side. When I had once again settled in the middle lane, I let out the breath I had been holding and shouted, "It worked! I'll be damned, it worked!" Then I said, "Thank you, Holy Mother." I said it with extreme reverence, though I was pretty sure there had been no divine intervention. I thanked the car, too. "Thanks, Old Paint." And the wind returned with a vengeance.

The upshot of my planning was that I had no plan. I was going to barge in on J. P. Cosgrove, then act and react according to what I find there.

I almost missed my turnoff onto the William Floyd Parkway at Brookhaven. I screeched onto the exit from the center lane of the Expressway and, wouldn't you know it, damn near collided with the only other car in sight. A few minutes later, I looped onto Sunrise Highway for the last stretch of road to the Hamptons. Here the winds were stronger, but steadier; the highway was closer to the South shore, and quite deserted.

My mind toyed with a ghoulish puzzle.

Why was I still alive? But first I had to answer a prior question. *Was* I still alive? Could I conceivably be dead and only imagining I was driving my car through a raging storm? Or experiencing it in another dimension, some form of existence after life?

Crap, these were questions for a Philosophy 101 course, or the maunderings of a medieval monk. How many angels can dance on the head of a pin? Are you really there, or do you exist only in my mind?

The back of my head throbbed, and that was good enough for me. Q.E.D., I was still alive, albeit not as well as I could be. That brought me back to the original question: Why hadn't they killed me when I was unconscious on the floor of Alice's living room?

I could think of only two possibilities. Either they thought that the blow on the head *had* killed me, or they thought I didn't know enough to be a threat to them and was therefore not worth killing. A third possibility occurred to me: they intended to kill me but were interrupted, possibly by Alice herself. I kept thinking of a "they" as the intruders, but more likely it was a lone person who had followed me in. His first order of business had no doubt been to put me out of commission so he could handle Alice by himself. But he probably wasn't aware of her strength, and she had kept him so occupied with subduing her that he had had no chance to finish me off.

Ridiculously, I found myself snorting with rage. If they have harmed her, by God, I'll kill them all, every last murdering son of a bitch of them! I will! I will!

Yes, I will, damn it.

I drove down Mill Road off Montauk Highway. I knew Westhampton pretty well, having spent part of a summer there years ago. I didn't recognize Mill Road: The houses were different and old landmarks were gone. Tree branches blocked my way, and I had to go around them. At Main Street, the traffic light was still working and some of the stores appeared to be open.

I doglegged onto Beach Lane. Here the whole roadbed was covered with several inches of water, and I realized that the bay water had risen to this height. "Don't stall, old girl," I implored the car, "just don't stall."

A Jeep was plowing through the water from the opposite direction. A young guy lowered his window halfway and shouted, "They're not letting anyone through! Better turn around, feller."

"Who's stopping us?" I asked, the rain slashing me in the face.

"The Coast Guard. They're afraid the dunes will go."

I thanked him and drove on, determined that if the bridge to the beach was still intact, I was going to cross it.

But I couldn't. The roadblock was complete. There was no way of driving around it. Men in slickers were waving me to go back. One of them leaned toward my open window.

"No one's allowed through," he said. "The hurricane's about to hit, and we're the bull's-eye."

"But my wife and daughter . . ." I said.

"Probably evacuated. Try the church. Or the clubhouse off Potunk."

Potunk Lane. I nodded to him and turned back toward Main Street. I remembered we used to go down Potunk Lane to get to the other bridge, but I forgot the name of the last street leading to the bridge. I remembered that Main Street ended at Potunk. I saw now that most of the stores on Main were boarded up. I went down Potunk and headed down Jessup Lane. Somehow the car made the correct turns, though it had never been in Westhampton before in its life. Good girl, I said. That was it. Jessup Lane.

Close to the bridge was another roadblock, a looser one, thank God. Men with flashlights waggled at me and tried to jump in my path, but I steered the Escort onto someone's lawn and sped around the cars that were blocking the road.

Back on the road, I saw nothing but water between me and the hump of the bridge. Madness gripped me, a combination of rage and insanity. I talked to the car through gritted teeth. "Shit, you've gone through mud puddles deeper than this, old girl. Keep chugging, I said, no chugalug, no chugalug, y'hear, just chug." I kept my foot steady on the gas pedal, and the car barged through the axle-deep water, sending spray over the windshield.

Then we were on the bridge, where the wind tried to send us over the side. I promised the car rewards for making it to Cosgrove's cottage, just a measly mile west on Dune Road. I said, "How about an STP oil treatment. Wouldn't that be nice? And a car wash, not like this, but a real car wash with a hot wax bath and everything." Coming off the bridge, the car coughed, and I promised it a real garage, the most luxurious one on the West Side, no matter what it cost. And the car labored on.

Parts of Dune Road weren't as bad as the slope off the bridge, the parts where the dunes were high and private clubs like the Yardarm and Dune Deck cut down on the wind velocity. But the more open parts were a raging battlefield of wind and waves that broke over the lower dunes and cascaded across the road. I babbled to the car. "Hey, haven't we gone a mile yet, for God's sake? This has to be the longest mile in motoring history! Keep going, old girl!"

I recognized Cosgrove's cottage, not so much from the house itself as from the low dunes across the road. There was a saddlelike depression in them, a sort of valley that contained a footpath. Waves were thundering on the other side, and a torrent was sweeping through the valley and across the road. His was the only house that showed lights, apparently the only one whose occupants were still there.

By sheer guesswork and an act of faith, I turned into the semicircular driveway leading to the house, passing what appeared to be a large beach buggy that was parked in the drive facing the road. My valiant Escort chose that moment to give up the ghost. It coughed and went silent. Its momentum brought us to a halt beside two other cars in front of the house—a maroon Mercedes that I knew belonged to Cosgrove, and a smaller, sportier car that looked like an Audi.

I sat in the car for a moment, trying to collect myself. The car was rocking and shuddering in the blast of the storm. The roar filled my ears and dulled my brain. What now? Screwdriver. I got the screwdriver from the glove compartment. What else? Tire iron in the trunk, yes.

I opened the door of the car, and the wind took it and held it open. I edged out, and was immediately pinned to the open door. I felt I was drowning. How important is the damn tire iron? I asked myself. Very important, I decided. Clawing at the car, I pulled myself to the rear and managed to open the trunk, then found myself being tumbled into it.

Finally, clutching the metal tool as a bludgeon, I let the storm propel me out of control to the front door of the cottage. Braced against the frame of the doorway on both sides, I kicked at the door. The noise I made was lost in the roar of wind and surf. I kicked again and rattled the door, but no one came to open it. I thought briefly of returning to the car and sitting out the worst of the storm. I thought briefly of smashing at the door with the tire iron. But then my hand found the doorbell, and I jabbed at it. The last thing I expected to hear was the Avon chime. Dingdong. Symbol of middle-American gentility. I jabbed it again and again. Dingdong. Dingdong. I smiled grimly at the incongruity of it.

The door opened a crack, and a voice growled, "Who the bloody hell—"

I threw my weight at the door and, with the help of the gale, burst it open. A river of seawater flowed in with me. Stanhope clung to the door, getting soaked.

He said, "Now that you're in, you bloody bastard, help me close the flipping door."

I lent my weight to his, and we pushed the door closed. He stood there with his few strands of brown hair plastered to his skull, his white shirt and dark trousers sopping wet. He glared at me. We were standing in a small hallway.

He said, "I don't believe you are expected, sir."

"Just passing by," I said. "I've come to take Alice home. Where is she? Upstairs, or in here?" Still clutching the tire iron, I moved quickly through a doorway into a small living room.

Behind me, Stanhope announced, "Mr. Carey was just passing by, sir."

The room was a cozy bit of old New England. The master of the house was seated in a rocking chair, with a reading lamp near his left shoulder. He was wearing what I believe is called a smoking jacket. His two guests, a man and a woman, were perched in a love seat near the fieldstone fireplace, looking at me expectantly. The rosy fire in the fireplace was the most attractive feature to a drenched and thoroughly chilled newcomer. Above the fireplace was a rack for holding a shotgun, or in earlier days a musket, but the gun was missing. It was cradled in the lap of the master, and aimed directly at me.

13

I said, "I won't be long. I've just come to get Alice."
The silence that ensued was unnerving.
I looked down at the tire iron in my hand.
"Oh, that," I said with a laugh. "My car was afflicted with a flat just outside your house, J. P. I started to put on the spare, but in this weather . . ." I let my voice trail off.
The silence wasn't complete, of course, but in here the sounds of the storm were relatively muted and were mingled with the rattles and creaks of the house.
Stanhope took the tire iron from my hand and stepped off to one side, apparently to get out of the line of fire from the shotgun.
"I bet you thought I was a looter," I said. "No need for the gun now. Just tell me where she is, and I'll go."
Finally, the great man of letters spoke. "Are you a hunter, Mr. Carey?" he asked, in those Boston Ivy League tones.
"No. No, I'm not," I said earnestly. "Somehow, killing animals never appealed to me. But I'm sure it's a great sport."

"Pity," Cosgrove said. "Then you wouldn't know the difference between a bird gun and a varmint gun. This is a bird gun, a 20-gauge Ruger Red Label, one of the finest for the money. But though it's a bird gun, I use it to shoot varmint. You'd be surprised at the number of rats there are in the marshes here. At close range, they sort of just . . . disintegrate."

I was cold, wet, exhausted, and beyond fright. My madness gave me a form of fatalism, in which I could go through the motions of the role I had elected to play—without hope, however—knowing that I had probably blundered into the endgame of my ineffectual existence, yet able to make the moves that would delay, I hoped, the inevitable outcome.

"I get the message, you pompous old fart," I said. "If you're calling me a varmint, shoot whenever the hell you feel like. It's the only way you're going to stop me from finding Alice."

I turned my back on him, feeling a tingling in the back where the blast would hit. I was already convinced that Alice wasn't here, but I had to make sure.

The man on the love seat stood up, as if to stop me.

I said, "Don't do it, David."

I'm sure it wasn't my threat that made David Glass stop; more likely, it was a gesture from Cosgrove behind me.

I looked at the woman, who had remained seated. "Where is she, Honor?" I asked.

Honor O'Toole shook her head. "I don't know what you're talking about," she said without her usual forced gaiety. The laugh lines on the lovely face now showed themselves to be age lines.

I moved out into the hall and up the stairs. It didn't take me long to check the three bedrooms and bath. No Alice, no corpse in the closet, no sign that she had been there. Up here, the structure was swaying more noticeably; the window in the front bedroom had been shattered by a flying oar, and the wind blasted through to the back rooms with a fierce spray of water pellets.

I went down the stairs and into the living room.

"You're going to lose your roof, J. P." I said.

"Nonsense." He was still seated in the rocker, with the shotgun pointed at me. "This house is solid as a rock. It's been through hurricanes before, and never lost a shingle. The hurricane doesn't exist that can budge this house."

Honor O'Toole stood up just as a particularly vicious gust made the room sway, and she almost fell back down on the seat. "I sure hope you're right, Mr. Cosgrove," she said. "I need a drink. Anybody else?"

I said, "Jameson on the rocks, Honor, please."

She looked at Cosgrove, and he nodded benignly. The old son of a bitch was playing a game with me, and enjoying it immensely. Honor went into the back room, which I took to be the kitchen.

I said to Cosgrove, "Is Jameson your favorite whiskey?"

He nodded. "That and Bushmill's," he said.

I said, "Mind if I sit?" Before he could answer, I sat down in a straight-back chair.

I smiled at him. I said, "One of your mistakes was assuming that all Irishmen like Irish whiskey. They don't. Take Father Frank Garvin, for instance. He loved the spirits dearly, but he couldn't stand the taste of Irish. And yet he was found with an empty bottle of Jameson. Isn't that curious?"

The old man glanced at David Glass, who said, "Blame Uncle Will. Don't blame me."

I said, "Who's Uncle Will?"

Cosgrove said, "That's neither here nor there. The question is, what should we do with a renegade Irishman?"

"Only half Irish," I said brightly. I felt I had to keep talking, like Scheherazade, to hold off the moment of my demise.

"What's the other half?"

"English."

The great ugly head nodded. "Of course," Cosgrove said.

"It explains my schizophrenia," I said, sliding into the role of clown. "One side of me is constantly at war with the other. One side shoots rubber bullets, and the other throws hand grenades. It keeps me awake nights."

The old man tightened his grip on the gun. "Right now you're shooting rubber bullets, Carey," he said. "The English part has its boot on the Irish part's neck and is crushing it, just as they're doing in Ulster. What was your mother's maiden name?"

"Atkins. Agnes Atkins."

"Perfect," he said. "For the time being, you are Atkins. Tommy Atkins. That's more appropriate, don't you think?"

Honor O'Toole brought me my drink, and I thanked her.

I said, "It sounds strange to my ears. I have an uncle named Thomas Atkins. He's an old man now, but I'm sure he won't mind you calling me by his name."

I raised my glass in a toast. "To peace in Northern Ireland." The whiskey did strange things to my stomach.

"Not peace, Atkins. Victory." He had a glass with the remnants of a soft drink in it, which he put to his mouth.

Suddenly, David Glass was between us, grabbing at the gun in Cosgrove's lap. "How long is this junk gonna go on?" he cried. "Let me finish him off for you."

Then Stanhope was behind Glass, with a hand on the cartoonist's bony shoulder. "Easy does it, young man," he said.

I made it to the front door and was fumbling with the latch when I realized that the large butler was now behind me. "Not yet, Mr. Carey," he said. "Perhaps later. Shall we return to the living room?"

The door quivered violently, and water perked beneath

it into the hall. I realized I wouldn't last two minutes out there in the storm; my life expectancy in the living room was maybe a bit longer, depending on the master's mood.

"Good idea," I said, and preceded him back into the room.

Cosgrove said, "That was dumb, Atkins. Just as we were drinking a toast, too."

I was sick and tired of his supercilious gab. "There is no victory, you phony bastard," I said. "It's that kind of thinking that keeps the killing going. And in your push for victory, you kill indiscriminately, not only British soldiers and Protestant Irishmen, but even full-blooded Irish-Americans who are sympathetic to the cause—like Tom Costigan."

Cosgrove waggled the gun. "Sit down, Tommy Atkins," he said. "I don't like you moving about like that. It makes my trigger finger nervous. . . . There, that's better. We can discuss the traitor Costigan if you wish, but before we do, I'm mildly curious why, in your primitive mind, you consider me a 'phony bastard.' I can understand the bastard part, but I don't understand why that makes me a phony. Please elucidate."

"Elucidate!" I whooped. "I love the word. It's pure Cosgrove. . . . Forgive me for chortling with English glee," I said more soberly. "Why do I call you phony—let me count the ways. In the first place, you write columns of opinion which presume to be vast words of wisdom but are in fact half-assed at best and worthless tripe most of the time. The only person in the whole world who likes them is Horace Hawthorne, who is an empty-headed son of a rich man—"

"He *is* empty-headed, isn't he?" Cosgrove said. "Thank God for that. But what you've said doesn't make me a phony. I'm quite sincere, believe me."

"Okay, I believe you," I said. "Cross out point number one. Point two, in all your novels you pose as an in member of the New England elite who is gently poking fun at the morals and traditions of your fellow plutocrats and their snooty wives. But you're not poking fun, are you? You're attacking them viciously; you're practically blowing them apart with your verbal grenades. And you're not a member of the upper crust at all, are you? What were your folks, J. P.? Shanty Irish? Bog-trotters who never had an indoor privy?"

David Glass was trembling. "How can you sit there and let him—"

Cosgrove said calmly, "His time is coming, David. Don't be in such a rush. It appears that we have a storm to wait out before our friends get here." He held out his glass. "Miss O'Toole, will you do the honors?"

I glanced at Honor's face just in time to catch the look of resentment at this male assumption that woman's lot was that of cook and barmaid. The look vanished, and she jumped to her feet. "Glad to," she said. The body was just as shapely in cashmere sweater and skirt as it always was in her skimpy blouses, but my libido failed to respond. I wondered whether I was growing up or growing old, or whether the near prospect of death canceled all normal responses.

I said, "What's that you're drinking, J. P.?"

He made a face. "Tab," he said.

I gasped in mock shock. "You drank a toast to your beloved Ireland with . . . *Tab?*"

Suddenly, the brows and mouth on the great horse face knotted and the whole visage darkened. I thought it strange that of all the insults I had heaped upon him, it was this one that struck home. I watched the muzzle of the gun waver, and I thought, Here I come, Lord, ready or not. *Oh, my God, I am heartily sorry . . .*

The critical moment passed, and Cosgrove said, "You really are a snotty prick, aren't you? I drink Tab on the advice of my doctor. I don't have a death wish, as you seem to have, Atkins. It's the intention that counts in a toast, not the alcoholic content. Now, where were we? Oh, yes, 'shanty Irish.' That's the Englishman in you talking, my dear young squirt. But yes, I guess you could call us that. We lived near Scollay Square, but I learned all about Beacon Hill doings from my mother, who was a maid in their miserable, suffocating homes. No matter how far they were separated in time and distance from their homeland, they were still English, damn them to hell! They were originally colonists, but not anymore. They stole their wealth from the Indians and from the black skins of the slaves they ripped from Africa and transported in their ships, and with their stolen wealth they created an inbreeding aristocracy that was closed to all others, especially the Irish. 'No Irish need apply'; you've heard of those words, Atkins. The Irish were only good enough to be laborers and housemaids. And so my father was a laborer in a mill, and my mother was a slavey who cleaned up their slop. Yes, we were shanty Irish, and proud of it!"

I said, "But not too proud to pose as a Brahmin yourself."

"If that was the way to bring about their destruction, yes," Cosgrove retorted. "It's the story of Ireland all over again, the English with the whip hand and the Irishmen kept in their place. Divide and conquer. So they've kept Ireland divided for three hundred years. But now their time has run out. They're about to be blasted off Irish soil, and maybe then the Irishman will be the master and the groveling Englishman his servant. A fitting turnabout, don't you think?"

I peered around the room. "Hey, Stanhope, where are you?" I saw him standing by the door behind me. "Is that why you're serving Lord Cosgrove here? Did he find you groveling, and take you in to clean up his slop?"

The tall butler glanced at me as if I were a pile of ripe garbage.

Cosgrove started to say, "Is there no end—" but two occurrences stopped his words.

David Glass, with an inarticulate cry, leaped to the fireplace and snatched up a poker.

And the lights went out.

Glass stood over me with upraised poker. What light

there was in the room was that of late dusk, which flickered with the movement of wind and foam outside the window. As if to emphasize its furious power, a monumental surge of water crashed against the house and caused it to move.

Honor O'Toole got to her feet and was immediately thrown back down. "Holy Mother of God, the house is breaking up! We're going to drown!"

"Nonsense!" Cosgrove said. "Everyone simmer down. The house is safe."

I tried to move, but Stanhope had me by the shoulders and held me down. Glass was still poised over me with the poker.

Cosgrove said, "David, put that ridiculous thing where it belongs. Stanhope, light the lamp."

I felt the hands leave my shoulders, and watched Cosgrove's manservant go to the mantel and light the hurricane lamp that was there.

The new yellowish light had a quieting effect.

Honor O'Toole started to weep softly. "I came out here to plead for no more killings, and now we're all going to be killed by the storm. What do you call that, Eddie? Ironic, is that the word? I never had your education. We kill a sweet and gentle man for no good reason, and God turns around and blasts us with a hurricane."

"Ironic is a good enough word," I said. "Especially since the hurricane is named Colleen. Another expression you might use, in honor of Brendan, is poetic justice."

"Poetic justice, my foot," Cosgrove announced. "I'm afraid Miss O'Toole has had a bit too much to drink, that's all."

I kept my eyes on the woman. "I loved Max, too," I said. "Who killed him?"

She glanced at David Glass and turned away. "A certain crazy individual," she said, "and his—"

The young cartoonist interrupted and overrode her words. "She's drunk, Father," he said to me. "I can't stand drunken women. They're... they're..." He searched for words that didn't come.

I said, "You puzzle me, David. I never thought of Glass as an Irish name."

"That shows how much you know," he said. "I'm Irish. My father and mother came from Dublin. They were born there. I'm as Irish as—"

"Leopold Bloom," I interjected. "That's it. Now I have it. You're an Irish Jew."

Through clenched jaws, he said, "I won't dignify you by talking to you. I'll say no more."

"You're a convert," I said. "And like all converts, you have to be more Irish than Robert Emmet. Did you have fun killing a fellow Jew?"

He sat rigidly, not looking at me.

Cosgrove said in a tired voice, "You persist in being unpleasant, Mr. Atkins. I think I must ask you to keep quiet. I really don't want to soil the carpet with your blood, but I will if you push me."

"Would you really kill me just for opening my mouth?"

"Keep it up, and see." The faded blue eyes made it appear as if there were nothing in the skull but a vast empty space.

"That's murder," I said.

"Wrong. It's disposing of a limey rat. I have a license to kill varmint."

A wall of water slammed into the front of the house, and a moment later the front window exploded outward. Then a juggernaut of water drove through, toppled the love seat, sending David Glass and Honor O'Toole over backward, and smothered the fire with a great hissing and billowing of black smoke. The water swirled around my feet.

Cosgrove still sat in his rocker, drenched with spray. He said, "Help them, Stanhope." And the butler pulled the young guests to their feet.

"Everyone to the kitchen," Cosgrove said, herding us through the door to the back of the house. "Take your chair with you, Atkins. It's a kitchen chair anyway."

The moiling water in the kitchen was a foot deep, but we were out of the direct brunt of wind and wave.

"Well, now," Cosgrove said. "They have breached our battlement, we have taken their best shot, and they have failed! We're safe in here. A little uncomfortable, but safe."

As if to bear out his words, the terrible wind suddenly died, the light outside the window grew brighter, and in a moment there was hazy sunlight.

"There! What did I tell you!" Cosgrove crowed. "This stout old house has weathered another storm and come out triumphant."

He looked at me. "I am feeling magnanimous, Atkins. You seem to have lost your drink. Make him another, Miss O'Toole. The condemned man needs a little last-minute cheer."

"Make it bourbon, if you will, Honor honey," I said. "I'm not worthy to drink Irish."

"Whatever he wants," Cosgrove said.

We were seated around the kitchen table, Cosgrove a little away from it so that he could still hold the shotgun in his lap. The waves continued to pound the house and the water swirled around our legs, but the wind was still, and the house was bathed in misty, late-afternoon sunlight.

I said, "Since I *am* a condemned man, I believe I'm entitled to ask a few questions in lieu of a last meal."

"Ask away," Cosgrove said. The smile on his face made me want to smash it.

"Where's Alice Costigan?"

"She's in protective custody. She's safe, for the time being. That's all you need to know."

"Where?"

"A stone's throw from where she was taken."

"How do you know? You were on your way out here at the time."

"Haven't you heard of the telephone, Atkins? It's a new invention—"

"I've heard of the telephone," I said. "Is she going to be brought out here?"

"As soon as the storm is over." Cosgrove looked at his

watch. "They are undoubtedly starting out now, even as we speak."

"Why?"

"Why what?"

"Why is she being brought here?"

"Well, now, I'm afraid that the young lady knows too much, and being her father's daughter, she's an enemy of the revolution. What was the expression Mr. Ehrlichman used during Watergate? Deep-six. I do believe that someone is going to deep-six her."

"From your boat?"

He nodded. "From my boat. It's possible you may meet a similar fate. How very romantic, don't you think? The two lovers drowned in the same storm. A reenactment of the story of Hero and Leander."

I said, "I think I'm going to be sick."

Honor O'Toole pounded a fist on the table. "That's the whole point!" she said. "Why does there have to be more killing? Eddie doesn't have any proof against us, do you, Eddie? You're not going to rat to the police, are you?"

"Of course not," I said.

"And that holy Costigan woman," Honor went on. "She has nothing. Why don't we just forget the whole thing? Get out of this business. We've done our share. More than our share. Let someone else get guns for our fighting men, and money for the cause. There are plenty of patriots around. Why don't we just get out? That way, even if Eddie does go to the police, they won't be able to do a thing to us. And we won't have to kill anymore."

"I second the motion!" I said. "Let's put it to a vote. The way I see it, there will be two for the motion, and two against. That would leave the deciding vote in the hands of Stanhope."

I looked up at Stanhope, who was standing near the back door. "Be honest now, Stanhope," I said. "Would you want the terrorists who are the enemies of England to have an atomic device that could kill a hundred million of your people? I'm not out to put anyone in jail. I don't care if Mr. Cosgrove raises money and arms for the IRA. I think the history of England in Ireland, from Cromwell on down, is a disgrace, and the only way they're going to get out is to be shoved out.... David, you said it was a war, and my fiancé compared the IRA to the Mau Mau in Kenya. Okay, I buy that. It's guerrilla warfare, and war is hell, and all that. But I do object to the killings that have been going on here not to win the war, but to silence innocent people who stumble on your secret. And I most strongly object to putting an atom bomb in the hands of madmen, because that's what the Provisionals are—madmen. So how do you vote, Stanhope?"

The tall man's face was expressionless. "There aren't a hundred million people in all of the United Kingdom," he said.

"Okay, let's say a million Englishmen. How do you vote?"

"I vote for the man with the gun," he said.

"Suppose Cosgrove didn't have a gun. How would you vote then?"

He said, "Before I came to serve Mr. Cosgrove, I was a valet to English gentry. My father before me was a valet, and my mother was a maid. It was a form of slavery. Does that answer your question?"

"No," I said.

"Enough," Cosgrove said. He had been listening to our words with an amused look on his face. Apparently, we had ceased to amuse him. "You've had your say, Carey, and you have failed to convert anyone to your pitiful stand, not even our tipsy Miss O'Toole. Now it's time for more serious discussion. Stanhope, my stout fellow, what can you rustle up in the way of food? I'm famished."

Stanhope, from the larder, said, "Most of it is spoiled, I'm sorry to say."

"Well, get something—anything. I'm not on a hunger strike like the immortal Bobby Sands and the others—"

"The immortal Bobby Sands!" I exclaimed. "I must be English, after all, because I don't understand the Irish.

They claim that they're Catholic, and yet they say that what Bobby Sands did was a great and noble act. But do you know what he did? He committed suicide! He committed suicide by starvation. One of the greatest sins in the Church's roster of sins! And yet they treat him as a hero. Can you explain that to me, J. P.? Or aren't you a student of the Church's teachings?"

Cosgrove nodded disdainfully. "You're English," he pronounced, then said, "What have you got for us, Stanhope?"

"How about some bread and cheese, sir?"

"A magnificent collation," Cosgrove said. "Bring it forth, my good and faithful servant."

I said, "Do I still have some questions coming to me, J. P.? I promise not to be offensive. At least I'll try."

"Go ahead, you tiresome fellow. Ask what you will, but I don't promise you'll get answers. Ah, thank you, Stanhope. Good man."

As the old man nibbled on a cheese sandwich as if it were a caviar canapé, I said, "Several things puzzle me, but they all come down to one question: who was the actual murderer? Or murderers, I should say, because I believe that at least two of the killings were done by more than one person. For instance, I know for a fact, or almost know for a fact, that two men killed poor Danny Dunn, and that one of those men was our young, hotheaded patriot here, David Glass. The more I look at you, David, the more I realize—from your posture, the way you carry yourself—that you were one of the men I saw walking away from Danny's body. And the way you walked, you may have been carrying something, but I couldn't make it out. Was it your machete, David? Did you slit Danny's throat with one snick of your murderous machete?"

A jumble of emotions showed on the young man's face, but he maintained a sullen silence.

"You were right, J. P.," I said. "You didn't promise me answers. Okay, the other killing that was done by two men, according to the way I figure it, was the suicide of Max Abel. And again, one of the murderers had to be the selfsame David Glass. Honor said it was a certain crazy individual, and that seems to fit you, David, no offense intended."

The cartoonist's hands were crushing a cheese sandwich.

I said, "Let the record show that Mr. Glass does not respond."

Cosgrove said, "You're boring us. . . . Stanhope, can you see the boathouse from there? How is it standing up?"

Stanhope peered out the back window and said, "It's still there, sir."

I went on as if there had been no interruption. "But the murder that puzzles me the most is Costigan's. All three of you were there at the syndicate party. J. P., you were the guest of honor. Hail to the great author, and all that. Honor, you were there with Max. Oh, he was so proud of you. You made him feel like a youngster all over again—"

Honor said, "Eddie, please!"

"It's true, honey," I said. "You were there too, David, spreading your usual measure of good cheer. If one of you three was the killer, it had to be you."

David said, "You're crazy."

"But I don't think you did it," I said. "Do you want to know why?"

"No."

"Because you had no place to hide the grenade. If it were stuffed in your pocket, we all would have noticed. So none of you could have killed Tom Costigan. Isn't that nice?"

None of them responded, and I saw I was losing my audience.

"But there were two other interested guests at the tavern that night," I went on. "In the restaurant. One was Joey Gargano, who had a motive. Tom Costigan was wrecking one of his rackets. Ordinarily a pretty good motive, but in this particular case, the wrong motive.

Tom wasn't killed by the Italian Mafia, he was killed by the Irish Mafia. I can give you my reasoning for that, if you want to hear it."

David Glass yawned. Honor O'Toole had a glazed look in her eyes. Cosgrove turned in his chair and said, "Stanhope, if you can get to the boathouse, look in and see if the boat is all right, like a good fellow."

Stanhope went out the back door. Discounting Honor O'Toole as a factor, that left me facing an old man with a shotgun and an unpredictable young man who was unarmed. The odds against me had shortened.

I pondered this as I went on speaking. "So that leaves the Poet Laureate of Hibernia by way of Hell's Kitchen as the probable bomb thrower. An unlikely role for a poet, I agree, but then Brendan Power is an unlikely poet. His 'Ballad to Bobby Sands' is the worst piece of trash I ever heard. And wasn't it a strange coincidence that he was at the Tom Jones Tavern that night? I'll bet he'd never been there before. An Irish patriot like him wouldn't be found dead in an English-style pub unless he had a reason for going there."

Cosgrove was dividing his attention between me and the back door. The other two were sunk in sullen apathy. Now was the time to make my move, I decided.

The sunlight suddenly vanished, and a great gust of wind walloped the house.

"Honor, you're a close friend of Brendan's," I started to say. Then, as the realization hit me, I blurted out, "Son of a gun, that was the eye of the storm that just went over us! J. P., you stupid old asshole, the storm isn't over! It was just catching its breath. Here it comes again!"

I stood up, gripped the edge of the table, and shoved it with all the force I had at the old man, slamming it into his stomach, trapping the shotgun on his lap beneath it. He started to go over backward, and the sound of the shotgun's detonation seemed to bulge the room. Cosgrove was on his back in the water, and I was scrambling toward him with the idea of getting possession of the gun.

A renewed surge of water from the living room doorway made me lose my footing and crack my head on the stove.

I was sprawled in the water. David Glass was standing over me with the shotgun. From the look on his face, I knew that nothing on earth was going to stop him from squeezing the trigger.

I cried, "Not yet," hoping for an extra fraction of a second. I tangled my feet with his and kicked him off balance. The shotgun blast was deafening. My face was under the salt water, and I was gulping it into my lungs. If I was hit, I felt no pain.

The water was tumbling me about. I got my head above it and was slapped in the face by a wave. I frantically wiped the water from my eyes. Cosgrove was struggling to sit up, his breath making a rasping sound. I don't know if I had toppled David Glass or not; in either case, he was on his feet, shooting me again and again with the empty shotgun.

I looked for Honor O'Toole. At first, I didn't see her. Then I saw her lovely face, barely above water, the upper part of her body resting on an overturned chair. I was about to speak to her when I noticed the startled look frozen on her face. As I gaped, a swirl of water momentarily revealed the breast and torso that had caused in me many a fitful dream. In the words of Cosgrove, her whole midsection had just sort of disintegrated. Then the waters covered her.

I felt terminally cold, and I wondered if I, too, were similarly disintegrated.

David Glass was coming at me, swinging the shotgun. It hit the side of my head, and a great roaring filled my universe, an internal clamor combining with the din of the storm. I went under.

14

This son of a thick-headed Mick never lost awareness. Not completely. I knew—hazily—that I had to get my head above water. I felt the butt of the shotgun slam into my shoulder, the fleshy part, and pictured David Glass chopping with the gun in a blind frenzy. I thrashed about in my own frenzy to keep from drowning. Only after I was coughing and gagging—and breathing air!—did I realize that the blows had ceased.

I heard the labored breathing of J. P. Cosgrove. Then I heard him gasp, "David ... the nitroglycerin ... there." For an instant, I thought he was going to blow up the house before the storm demolished it, and I thought that was wildly funny. Then I remembered his heart attacks.

Apparently, David found the medicine somewhere in a cabinet, because the next thing I heard was Cosgrove speaking more normally, but so weakly that I could scarcely hear him.

"No gun. A drowning ... David, listen to me. The back door ... open it. ... I'll hold the gun. ... Give it to me, David ... Good ... Now, just float him ... out the door."

I tried to get on my hands and knees. It was apparent that Stanhope had been caught in the renewed storm and hadn't returned. If a strong man like him could be swept away, I knew that my chances of survival were small. The water undermined my efforts.

Hands grabbed me, and I said again, "Not yet." Then I was out the door and being tumbled about in turbulent water, spinning, trying to get my feet under me, and being slammed sideways. I would like to say that my last thoughts were about Alice and how I had failed her, and how her name was similar to my mother's and that was the reason I could love her as sweetheart, wife, and mother. But I didn't think of Alice at all. I thought about my bursting lungs and my ridiculous inability to get to my feet and the rage I felt at being so helpless.

I stopped struggling and let the water take me. I let the air out of my lungs, resigned to death.

My body slammed against something hard, and without consciously wishing it, I resumed the struggle to get to my feet. My back was against the boathouse and my head above water. My hands clutched at the shingle siding to keep from being swept on into Moriches Bay, and my feet pushed me erect. I clung to the boathouse, buffeted by wind and ocean . . . God, yes, that was what I was standing in, the *ocean!* I saw that the valley in the dune across the road was now a full-fledged inlet!

The boathouse was not directly behind Cosgrove's cottage, but rather directly behind the entrance driveway in which the large dune buggy had been parked. But the buggy wasn't there anymore. It was beside me, having been inched backward by the forces of the storm until it had been halted by the boathouse. In the semidarkness, I saw that the gap in the dune was narrow and that the full power of the ocean was hitting the cottage but not the boathouse.

The pummeling was sapping my strength, and if I stayed where I was, I would surely be washed into the bay. I peered at the vehicle and saw that it wasn't a dune buggy at all but a GMC Jimmy with balloon tires—apparently J. P.'s condescending attempt to appear as one of the common folk, using the Jimmy as others would use a pickup truck for local hauling. It was jammed against the doorway to the boathouse, preventing me from seeking dubious refuge inside.

"Okay, Jimmy old boy," I muttered. "You're it."

Getting into the car exhausted all my remaining strength. Each time I opened the door an inch, a gust or wave slammed it shut. I finally succeeded in placing my body in the opening. I waited while the elements tried to squeeze the life out of me, then, with desperate lunges, made it inside. I lay across the front seat for several minutes, while the wind rocked the car insanely as if raging at my escape. Then I sat up behind the wheel.

It was from this blurry vantage that I saw the destruction of J. P.'s cottage. It wasn't the hurricane itself that did it. Cosgrove had been right about that: in all likelihood, his house would have survived the onslaught of air and water. But he hadn't foreseen that the storm would use battering rams—the three cars parked in front of the house.

I saw the mammoth wave coming. I could see the rears of the cars around the front corner of the house. The Audi went first. I heard the impact, the splintering. Then the Escort, my lovely Escort. Wham. But the coup de grâce was administered by J. P.'s bulky status symbol, the Mercedes. It must have rammed into the key support beam, for the house collapsed backward, not fast like a house of cards but slowly like something in a psychedelic dream. Succeeding waves toyed with it, tossed the various pieces about, and then the cottage wasn't there anymore, only the cars snagged on the pilings. There were no signs of human forms in the froth and foam.

I had no time for rueful thoughts. The Jimmy was being buffeted more strongly than before, thumping against the boathouse, splintering it. There are no atheists in a hurricane, and few agnostics. I prayed: *Holy Mary,*

Mother of God, pray for us sinners, now and at the hour of our death.

My hand found the key in the ignition switch—Glory be!—and my foot found the gas pedal. *Stick with me, Holy Mother; you're doing great so far.* I pumped the pedal and turned the key . . . and the starter whirred. It took a full thirty seconds, an eternity, for the motor to catch. It coughed, sputtered, then roared.

I don't know if I shouted or not. I had no time to let the motor warm up. The movement of the water gave me the queasy impression that I was moving backward. When I shifted into first, the first thing I realized was that the balloon tires were both a help and a hindrance. They had raised the engine high enough to keep it from shorting out, but the extra inflation made them act like pontoons. They wanted to float!

The car spun its wheels and fishtailed wildly. My foot was too heavy on the pedal. I let up halfway, and slowly we started toward the driveway, where the treads got a bit more purchase and gave me the illusion that I was in control of the vehicle.

The wind, now sweeping from the west, played with the wipers, at one moment forcing them away from the windshield to fan ineffectually in the downpour, and the next letting them snap back to give me fractions of moments of the view ahead. The car slithered and slewed until I found the switch to shift it into four-wheel drive. Progress out of the driveway was slow, then disastrously fast when the spinning wheels hit the roadbed and spurted ahead, almost plunging us into the sand on the other side of the road.

I headed east on a road I couldn't see, and at a speed that was much faster than I could control because the wind was now propelling the car from the rear. I steered the car frantically to compensate for the vagaries of the wind, staring through the blurry curtain of water to catch a glimpse of the next utility pole in the file of them that ran parallel to the road, only to find that some of them were down and the gaps seemed to be measured in light years. The only reason I made it to the bridge was that the unseen road was straight, and the Virgin Mother was looking out for me. Had to be.

Making the left turn onto the bridge almost brought disaster. The wind, hitting the car broadside, rammed it sideways into the guardrail; for a breathless moment, the car was tilted on its two right wheels and seemed about to be toppled over the rail and into the bay. There was a grinding of metal. . . . Then the car righted itself, and I let out my breath. We bounced against the rail two more times before we got to the other side.

"We made it, Jim boy," I said weakly.

I had forgotten about the roadblock. My mind had gone blank. Automatically, thoughtlessly, I brought the car to a halt, and a man in rain gear rapped on the window. I opened it halfway.

"Where in hell did you come from?" he asked, hunched against the pounding rain.

My mind groped for an answer. If I blurted out the whole truth, I knew I would be detained—delayed from something urgent that was pulling me back to the city. Yet I was in Cosgrove's car, and I had to give an explanation of that.

I said, "J. P. Cosgrove . . . the writer . . . he and his guests are in his cottage . . . The dune across the road gave way . . . Sent me to get help . . . Not in danger yet, but—"

"Damn fools," the man said. "Where are they?"

"A mile east," I said. "Bay side. Cape Cod. Gray. Can't miss it."

"Shit," the man said. "You'll have to show us, feller. Pull over there."

"Gotta get to the hospital," I said. "Surely someone here must know the Cosgrove place."

The man frowned, peered into the rear of the Jimmy, then turned and called out: "Hey, Grover. Know the Cosgrove place?"

Another hunched-over figure approached. "Cosgrove? J. P. Cosgrove? The place he calls 'Sea Shanty'?"

"That's the one," I said. I hadn't recalled the cute appellation, but it sounded like J. P. "Better get to him quick. I don't know whether the house can hold out."

The first man said "Shit" again, and they moved away.

I gunned the motor, almost stalling it, and drove around the roadblock. I found Mill Road and headed toward the city. Hurricane Colleen swirled around me, having lost none of her force.

The ghostly flashes of light on the road ahead fascinated me. I had heard of this sort of apparition over swamps, but not over roadbeds. I slowed down. The bluish lights flickered not only on the road but seemed to bathe a stalled car with their glow. When I saw the writhing snake, I knew what it was. A downed electric line. I jammed on the brakes and caught a glimpse of the stalled car's driver, quivering in the pale light.

I tried to pray for the poor guy, but I had to concentrate on backing the car and finding an alternate route to Montauk Highway.

Something had been digging into my side ever since I had gotten into the Jimmy, but I had been too busy to check it out. When I turned onto Sunrise Highway and the Jimmy was rolling west directly into the wind, I finally permitted my right hand to let go of the wheel and grope for the painful spot. The damned screwdriver! I had shoved the useless thing in my pocket and then forgotten about it. I took it out and laid it on the seat beside me. "What a knucklehead," I muttered in disgust.

The fuel gauge registered half a tank. There was no way I could conserve it, for I had to maintain a heavy foot on the pedal to keep going. There were gas stations on Sunrise Highway, I knew, but the chances were that they were all closed. I decided to move up to the Expressway, knowing it had no gas stations at all. The fuel that was in the Jimmy's tank had to get me through to Manhattan—and Alice.

My mind had shied away from thinking of her. Now,

as my struggles against the storm became more automatic, my mind zeroed in on her plight. That snide son of a bitch, the Bastard of Boston—now dead and sizzling in hell—had said she was "in protective custody." Protective custody, horseshit; she was kidnapped and held captive. My mind imagined the horrible things happening to her, my anger rose like lava, and I was slaughtering her kidnappers with David's machete, swinging it with righteous power, making the blood gush, gathering Alice into my mighty arms—

Suddenly, I was gaping at a true-life hallucination, and the mighty arms turned slack. A head had appeared in the rearview mirror. The head of a dead man. Cosgrove's man, Stanhope. Sparse hair wildly askew and tangled with seaweed, face deathly pale, eyes blazing. A face out of Dante's *Inferno*. I don't know how long I was transfixed by the awful apparition, but the spell was snapped when the face spoke.

"Watch where the bloody hell you're going!" it said.

I wrestled the car back onto the roadbed.

The apparition said, "What a bloody awful driver."

"Stanhope?" I asked in a voice that squeaked.

"In person, mate."

The face disappeared, and I heard a metallic clanking. Before I could figure out its meaning, something heavy flashed across my vision and tightened around my throat.

"No need for alarm, Mr. Carey," the voice said. "It's only a tow chain."

I gurgled something, and he loosened the chain enough to permit me to breathe.

"Sorry about that," he said. "I just wanted you to understand the situation."

The menace in the voice was unmistakable, but there was something else, a weakness that bespoke great physical fatigue.

I said, "So now the Englishman joins the Irish killers."

He said, "Keep driving."

The rain was diminishing, but the wind was still of

hurricane force, and I had to keep both hands on the steering wheel.

I said, "You went out to check on the boat. What happened?"

At first, I didn't think he was going to answer. Then he said in a tired voice, "This confounded motorcar pinned me to the boathouse. I couldn't get back to the house."

"But you managed to get in the car through the hatchback."

He didn't answer.

"And then you passed out," I said.

There was no reply from the back.

I remembered the guardsman at the roadblock peering into the back of the car. He must have seen Stanhope lying there and believed my statement that I was heading for a hospital. Otherwise, he would have asked more questions.

The face appeared once again in the rearview mirror.

I said, "Where are they hiding Alice Costigan?"

"That's nothing for you to worry about, sir," Stanhope said. He was staring straight ahead through the windshield. He said, "That overpass. Pull off and stop under it. It'll give us some shelter."

"For what?"

"I'm taking over. You're staying here."

I said, "Look, we're both going to the city. Why don't we go together? You can drive if you want. I promise not to try anything." I smiled my ingratiating smile, hoping he could see it.

"The city!" he said. "You bloody fool, I'm going back to help Mr. Cosgrove."

"You don't know, then?"

"What don't I know?"

"That J. P. is dead. The storm took all three of them, cottage and all."

The chain tightened viciously around my neck, and I heard a harsh laugh.

165

"Mr. Cosgrove was right, you *are* a snotty bahstard. And a piss-poor liar, to boot. *Here,* Mr. Carey."

I tried to speak, and couldn't.

I stopped the car in the lee of the overpass. There wasn't much protection from the storm. The wind simply struck from several directions at once. We were alone on the highway. There wasn't a car in sight in either direction.

"Good-bye, Mr. Carey," Stanhope said.

The chain dug into my throat. The large links were not ideal for garroting, but when I tried to pull the chain away with my hands, I couldn't. I twisted and struggled, and tightened my neck muscles against the strangling force. My right hand fell on the screwdriver, but there was no way I could wield it against the killer behind me. I had once seen an opossum play dead. It was at a friend's house upstate. We came upon it suddenly at dusk, and I could have sworn I was looking at a dead animal. When we backed away from it, however, it got up clumsily and waddled away. My last desperate chance now was to play possum.

I let my whole body go limp and my head loll to one side, my left hand trapped between the chain and my neck. I was losing consciousness fast. My diaphragm was contracting in spasms, and I willed it to stop. Darkness was creeping over my oxygen-starved brain. My mind was screeching to Stanhope, *I'm dead, you silly son of a bitch! Can't you see I'm dead, damn it! You can relax your grip now, I'm dead, I'm dead . . .*

And then I was. Dead.

First, some flashing lights, like a Grucci fireworks display. Then nothing. Blankness. No tunnel to eternity, no brilliance at the far end of it, no floating sensation, no guiding voices, no sound, sight, smell, or taste. No pain. No thoughts, no regrets. Nothing.

Rain whipped my face.

I heard a dog whimper.

I heard metal clank on metal.

I heard the blood hum in my veins, felt a pounding in my chest—and the dog whimpered again.

I opened my eyes and saw I was in a tunnel after all. Beneath an overpass, lying on the naked highway. I heard the *chunk* of a car door closing, and I stumbled to my feet. Gasping.

The hot rage returned. Cosgrove's turncoat Englishman was leaving me for dead, taking the car, *my* car! I had fought the storm and won the car that would take me to Alice, the prize of battle . . .

It was moving, Stanhope behind the wheel. I staggered to it, ripped open the door, grabbed his clothing, and fell backward, pulling Stanhope with me. The car veered, and crunched into the stone wall.

The two of us lay tangled on the cobblestone shoulder, the heavy Englishman on top. His knee slammed into my crotch without much force, but enough to send pain zinging through my body.

I threw him off, gained my feet, and staggered backward against the open door of the Jimmy. My hand reached back onto the front seat to push myself erect. It closed on the screwdriver.

The man came at me clumsily, a bull of a man somewhat weakened by his ordeal in the storm but still stronger than a man who had been recalled from death only seconds before. He lunged at me, his hands reaching for my neck; I tried to sidle away, and at the same time aimed my fist at the pit of his stomach, hoping it was not hard like an athlete's but soft like that of a butler.

He fell against me, and I scrambled toward the rear of the car to get away from him. He didn't follow. He stood by the open front door, swaying, his hands clasped to his stomach. It was then that I saw the yellow handle of my screwdriver protruding from his stomach.

I said, "My God!" and moved toward him with the instinctive idea of helping him. He backed away, moved sideways out into the open; then, as the hurricane wind caught him, he went reeling down the Expressway in the direction from which we had come—toward Westhampton and the cottage that wasn't there. I watched in shock as he somehow managed to put one leg in front of the other and remain erect before the propelling force of the wind. I knew it would be a matter of minutes at most before he went sprawling on the pavement. And he wouldn't get up. The chances were that he would die if I didn't help him.

I just stood there. My throat was a torture and my whole body ached, but the greatest agony was in my mind. I had just stabbed a human being, and who was to say the stabbing was accidental? After all, I had taken the screwdriver with me to use as a weapon, and the thought had to have still been there when I swung my fist at his stomach. I was responsible for his wound, and it was now my responsibility to try to save his life. If I did that, however, I would forfeit my chance of saving another life. Alice's.

As I stood there and watched the staggering figure disappear into the storm, I again heard the whimper of a dog. I moved toward the sound. The dog was lying on his side against the wall of the overpass. Motionless. A large dog with a reddish coat of long hair, he followed my movements with his eyes.

I squatted by him and put a soothing hand on his head. "You and me both, fella," I said.

He whimpered softly.

"You're in pain, aren't you?" I said. "Where does it hurt?"

I saw the gaping wound in his flank. I lightly touched his rib cage, and the dog swiveled his head as if to bite me.

"You're all busted up, aren't you?" I said. "Sorry."

I studied him for a moment. He was an Irish setter, obviously in great pain from broken bones and from the vicious wound in his side. How he came to be there was a mystery I had no way of solving. The fact was the dog was dying, and he was in pain.

In anguish I went to the Jimmy, found the compartment that held the spare tire and jack, and took out the tire iron. Another of my great lethal weapons!

I went back to the dog, patted him on the head, and said, "It's all I can do, old friend." And I brought the tire iron down on his head as hard as I could. . . .

I was sitting beside the dog, sobbing, plunged into a swirl of remorse and self-contempt so deep that I lost awareness of my surroundings. I was on trial for my life. . . .

"You're the one who's the vicious killer, Tommy Atkins." It was the voice of a dead author.

"Go away," I said.

The accusing voice said, "I may not be perfect, but I've never deliberately bashed in the skull of an innocent dog, I can tell you that."

I said, "He was in great pain, J. P., and he was going to die anyway. It was an act of mercy!" My God, I was pleading with him!

"Do you know for sure that he was going to die?"

I said, "When a horse breaks a leg, they—"

"This wasn't a horse, you murderous fellow, it was a dog, an Irish setter. You knew it was an Irish setter, didn't you?"

"Yes."

The voice said, "I rest my case."

Another voice said, "Tom Costigan for the defense, Your Honor."

I held my breath, waiting to hear the voice of God. I heard nothing but the wind of the hurricane far away.

Costigan said, "Why didn't you bash in the head of the butler?"

I said, "You don't do that to people. He wasn't necessarily going to die—"

Costigan said roughly, "He was going to die, and you know it! You stabbed him in the gut with a grimy screwdriver. . . . Have you ever been stabbed in the gut? No! Well, it's the worst pain a person can have. That butler was in terrible pain, and you let him wander off to die a lingering, horribly painful death—"

"Hey, whose side are you on, anyway?" I looked around, but couldn't see him.

Costigan said in a dead voice, "I've always hated you, Carey."

I heard Alice crying faintly from far off, "Help me, Eddie."

"Yes," I said, "I've got to help Alice." I resolved to stand up, but I remained sitting by the dead dog while I clambered out of the depths.

David Glass said, "It's war, Father." And the whiskey priest said in his piping voice, "And you're the battlefield, Edward."

I got to my feet. "That's right, it's war!" I said. "And the hell with all this! God, what a knucklehead!"

I staggered to the Jimmy. It was still in gear trying to push its way through the stone wall. The right front fender was crumpled, but not badly enough to cut into the tire.

I backed it away from the wall, said good-bye to the dog, and headed once more for the city. The hell with everything; I had to find Alice.

The wind was less fierce, the storm was moving away, and the car was able to make better time. The realization came to me that the storm may have ended in the city, and that Alice's captors may have already bundled her into a car and were driving her to the deadly rendezvous at Cosgrove's cottage. Cars were beginning to appear on the Expressway, but dusk had long since faded into darkness, and all I could see of the occasional cars were their headlights. There was no way I could catch a glimpse of the occupants to see if one of them was Brendan Power. I kept a heavy foot on the gas pedal and prayed that I had enough fuel to get us through the Midtown Tunnel.

15

I stopped on East Forty-second Street and put in a call to Lieutenant Fred Ferrante from a sidewalk booth. The wind was still blustery and the rain came in squalls; the streets of midtown Manhattan were eerily deserted. A bored male voice told me that Ferrante wasn't in his office and nobody knew when he was expected.

I hung up and slumped against the ledge beneath the phone. My throat seemed to be closing up, and I felt I was suffocating all over again.

I shoved aside the panic and dialed Alice's number, on the off chance she had been released and was home. I was going to let it ring a dozen times before I hung up.

A male voice answered on the second ring. "Yeah?"

"Sorry," I said. "Must've dialed the wrong number."

I started to hang up, when the voice said, "Who is this?"

I said, "Ferrante?"

He said, "Carey? Where the hell are you? I told you to stay here."

"Have you found Alice?"

"No, but—"

"This is a bad connection," I said. "I can hardly hear you. But tell me this, do you have the address of Brendan Power?"

"Carey, Carey, listen to me, you dumb bastard," Ferrante shouted. "You come straight here, you hear? It won't do you any good to go to Power's place. He isn't there."

"You searched the place?"

"Yeah. Listen—"

"No sign of Alice?"

"No. Listen. Trust us, Carey. We checked out all the names you gave us, and nobody's home."

"That's because . . ." I sighed deeply. "That's because they're all dead, except Power. The hurricane got J. P. Cosgrove, David Glass, and Honor O'Toole. Swept them right into the bay."

"What bay? What bay?"

"And Cosgrove's man Stanhope is wandering along the LIE with a screwdriver in his gut. Do you know of anybody else who was in on it?"

"Carey, Carey, you're not making sense. You come straight here, or I'll have you arrested."

"Nobody else?"

"Not yet. Listen—"

Suddenly my pitiful supply of energy drained away. Brendan Power was my last hope of finding Alice. I had no next move. In a dull voice, I said, "I'll be right there, Lieutenant."

"Good, good. Don't worry, Carey, we'll find your lady friend. Just get your ass up here pronto."

My mind dredged up some half-remembered words of Cosgrove's. I said, "How far can you throw a stone, Lieutenant?"

"Just come here, okay?" he said.

I said, "Okay."

I climbed back into the Jimmy. The gas gauge registered below empty. I drove crosstown on Forty-second. Anxiety was squeezing my stomach. I've lost, I thought; they're going to kill Alice, and I have no way of stopping them. And it's all my fault. I wasted hours going to the end of the island and back, when she was in Manhattan all the time. That's not just dumb, it's criminally dumb, for God's sake.

The motor conked out at Broadway and Forty-second Street. Times Square. The Crossroads of the World. I left the car there and started walking. Strangely, the porno movie houses were open for business, the esoteric arcades, the video parlors, head shops, and all the rest. And many of the regular denizens were there. Peculiarly, this air of monkey business-as-usual reassured me, loosened my mind long enough for me to remember.

A stone's throw from where she was taken.

How far can you throw a stone? Fifty yards? A hundred? What lay within a hundred yards of Alice's house? Other row houses, a few tenements, the dry cleaning place on the corner of Ninth. But why take the words all that literally? The expression is as imprecise as the prosaic "nearby," or the regional "spit and a holler."

I walked past Alice's house, counted my paces to the corner. Sixty-two. Sixty-two yards. Around the corner on Ninth was Vinnie's restaurant—not likely—and beyond it, Philbin's Irish Pub.

Philbin's.

Hangout of the last of the Irish-Americans remaining in Hell's Kitchen, the hyphenated patriots of Hibernia.

Even from the corner, it was obvious that Philbin's was closed. The overhanging sign with the neon shamrock was dark, swaying in the tailwinds of Colleen. The cars at the curb were tucked in and fast asleep....

I stood at the front door and peered in. A fifteen-watter glowed dimly over the cash register behind the bar. I felt as forlorn as the sight of the empty bar. My common sense and my deep fatigue told me to go back to Ferrante and leave everything to the cops. I had nothing to connect Billy Philbin to the IRA wild men—not solid Billy with the large capacity to listen to your woes and somehow make you feel better.

In the grip of indecision, I put my hand on the

doorknob and turned it. The door opened. Ridiculous. No bar owner in New York was stupid enough to leave the door unlocked. I pondered the possibilities and shrugged. Hell, here I was, and the door was open. I went in.

I eased the door closed, then, like a dummy, stood to one side so that I couldn't be seen from the street, which had no people in it. Cathedral silence pressed on me, without any of the echoing footsteps one hears at St. Patrick's. No sounds except the distant sounds of the fading storm. My mind said, *Get out, you jackass, before you're arrested.*

Peripheral vision caught furtive movement. I focused on the spot and saw a cockroach on the bar, a big, healthy fellow. Without thinking, I moved to it and flicked it off, then wiped the finger on my clothing as if it had been contaminated. *Get out.*

I gazed at the row of shillelaghs and wondered if they had ever been used in anger. My stomach growled, and I thought of food. The picture of Cosgrove nibbling on a cheese sandwich flashed in my mind. At least he didn't go hungry, I thought with pale ill will.

Okay, okay, I'm leaving, I said to myself. But I lingered. Listlessly. I had had a list, and I had used it up. I was disgusted with myself for thinking of a Tom Swifty at this moment of depression.

I turned to leave when I heard it. No more than a distant murmur. It might have been the wind, or a tenant in an upstairs room, or simply my imagination. Whatever. I couldn't leave now; I had to look.

I moved around the bar and pulled a shillelagh from its rack. I walked slowly to the rear, between tables. I tried the storeroom door. It was locked. Ridiculous. The front door was open, but the place where Philbin stored his pretzels and bar napkins was locked. Obviously, no one would be in there talking. Even so, I called "Alice" in a low voice. No answer.

I inched into the washrooms, men's and women's. Strong urine smell mingled with disinfectant, and nothing else.

In a dark alcove at the rear of the bar was the door to the basement. I stood by the door and heard nothing. Nuts.

I opened the door. Too carelessly. It made a creaking noise. Instead of the sepulchral darkness I had expected, I saw that the basement was illuminated with a yellowish light that spread to the open staircase.

A familiar voice said, "What was that?"

And another one, a mellifluous one, said, "A voice crying in the wilderness, the wind in the willow, the wail of the banshee, the creaking door to eternity—"

"Eternity, hell, it was the creaking door to the basement."

I stood frozen on the first step.

Hugh Mullen was peering up. "Well, saints preserve us, gentlemen!" he exclaimed. "Our prayers have been answered! It's the last of Margaret Thatcher's crew. Come on down, Eddie!"

I carried the club on my shoulder and tried to saunter down the stairs as devil-may-care as Cary Grant had strode through the horde of Kali worshippers in *Gunga Din,* and announced, "You're all under arrest!" What I planned to say was, "The jig is up, fellers, the place is surrounded." Or something like that.

It didn't come off. I cleared my throat, then stumbled on the third step from the bottom and fell into Mullen, clutching him to keep from falling, in the process of which I lost the shillelagh. His breath smelled strongly of whiskey.

Mullen chose to treat my encircling arms as an embrace. "I'm glad to see you too, Eddie my lad," he said, and I heard the melodious laugh of Brendan Power.

"So chummy of him to drop in," Power said. "Ask him to join us, Hugh."

I peered around in the light of the naked bulb that hung from a ceiling beam. Though the air was heavy with the smell of beer, the dimness and dampness reminded me of a cave, a pirate's cave. The great poet, in jeans and cable-knit sweater, posed languidly against stacked cases of Irish whiskey as I imagined an earlier compatriot, Oscar Wilde, might have posed, except that instead of a flower this poet held an automatic pistol. Pointed in my direction.

He said, "Innkeeper, offer the poor soul a drink. He looks like he could use it."

Billy Philbin sat on a barrel, his great arms folded across his chest. He said nothing, but his eyes exuded their usual somber sympathy for the sorry lot of mankind.

In the center of the open area was a large barrel that apparently served as a table. On it was an open bottle of Jameson and some glasses.

At first, I didn't see Alice. Then I saw her standing by the far wall at the perimeter of the dim light, standing like an embattled person with legs apart. In her hand she held a wooden mallet. Her pale-blue dress was rumpled, and torn at the shoulder; her hair was unkempt, and her face was smudged. As her eyes took me in, they changed from blazing defiance to a strange look of alternating hope and despair.

"Oh, Eddie," she wailed.

I gaped at her dumbly for a moment, then swiveled and slammed my fist into Mullen's stomach. He said, "Woof," just as they do in comic strips; he doubled over and sank to the cement floor. I kicked him, and was about to kick him again.

A quiet voice said, "That's enough, Eddie."

I turned around.

Philbin said, "If you do it again, Brendan will put a bullet in you." He was still seated, with arms folded.

The poet was uncharacteristically silent, but the gun was steady.

I said, "Sorry, Billy, but Mullen was closest."

"I know," Philbin said sympathetically.

I breathed deeply. "What skunk did that to Alice?"

Philbin shook his head in sorrow. "She's a tough lady, Eddie. She needed help in getting here."

"Bullshit," I said.

I went to Alice. She glared at me.

I said, "Let's sit down a moment. Then we'll get out of here." I took the bung starter from her hand and tossed it aside.

"You don't understand," she said. "They were just getting ready to take me someplace else. . . . They're going to kill us, Eddie!"

I hugged her shoulder. "I have a few things to say about that," I said. "Come on."

I moved two smaller barrels toward the center of the area. "Come on, sit."

We sat and faced our three captors. Mullen was still on the cement floor, stirring, making rasping sounds. Neither of the other two had moved to help him.

I said, "Who's in charge?"

I peered from one to another.

Brendan Power changed his pose. "Yours not to reason why, Carey. Yours but to do and die. You've done all the doing you're going to do, and now it's time for the dying." He moved toward me, acting like a movie gunman.

I said, "God, what a cornball! You're not going to shoot me, and you know it. Alice and I are going to drown, aren't we? And drowned people don't have bullet holes in them."

He swiped at me with the gun, and managed to hit the back of my head. The pain was sharp, but I rose to my feet, and he backed away quickly.

Alice cried, "Eddie!" and I became aware that another gun was trained on me. Mullen was sitting up. He had a gun in his hand.

I resumed my seat on the keg, trying not to show that my legs were weak.

Mullen said, breathing heavily, "Let's get out of here, goddamn it! The storm is over."

Brendan Power started, "O Captain! My Captain! Our fearful trip is done—"

"Shut up," Mullen said.

I said, "Yeah, shut up."

Mullen turned baleful eyes on me. "You, too, you sneaky bastard. I owe you one." He stood up. "Come on, gents. This place is a grave."

"If you'll forgive me for asking," I said. "What's the plan?"

Alice touched my arm. "The packing crate," she said. "If I don't come willingly, they're going to hit me on the head and put me in that."

I peered around. "And what about the bomb?"

Brendan Power, who had regained his jaunty composure, said, "Oh, we're taking it, never fear, we're taking it with us."

"What do you plan to do with it? Blow up Parliament?"

"Hey, that's a glorious idea," the poet said. "We'll pass on the suggestion."

I shook my head. "It won't happen, Brendan. You've missed the boat."

"Nonsense," he said. "We have our own private transportation."

"Not anymore you don't," I said. "I have a news bulletin for you. The eye of Colleen passed over Cosgrove's house. The house isn't there anymore. Neither is the boat. Neither is Cosgrove, for that matter. The poor man has been called to his reward. So has that crazy cartoonist, David Glass. So, I regret to say, has that gorgeous hunk of womanhood, Honor O'Toole. It's Colleen who's the traitor to the cause, not me or Alice."

Power laughed uncertainly.

Hugh Mullen glowered at me. "You don't mind if we go and see for ourselves, do you?" he said. "What are we waiting for?"

I glanced at Billy Philbin. He had an unhappy look on his face. It suddenly occurred to me that he might be there unwillingly, or at least reluctantly.

"Are you part of this, Billy?" I said to him. "Look at these two clowns! Just look at them! One of them is a stuffed English bulldog, and the other's a ridiculous pouter pigeon strutting around, saying, 'Coo,' and thinking he's reciting poetry. If they have some hold on you, the hell with it. Whatever it is, it can't be half as bad as going along with their madness. They're not patriots, they're crazy people who want to blow up civilization. If you say so, we can walk out of here, and be done with them. They're not going to use those peashooters. What do you say?"

Philbin's eyes moved from the squat figure of Mullen to the languid figure of the poet. "They *are* clowns, aren't they?" he said. His eyes returned to me. "But they are also patriots, Eddie," he said. "I disagree with you there. They're devoted to the cause of a united Ireland."

I let my shoulders slump. I had guessed wrong.

Brendan Power said quietly, "Thank you, Will."

"Oh, God," I muttered. Then I said, "Are you David's Uncle Will? The one who forced a bottle of Irish whiskey down Frank Garvin's throat?"

Philbin gazed at me with his infinitely sad eyes.

"We all do terrible things," he said, "knowing that we're going to hell. Knowing, too, that the Devil is an Englishman who will torture us for all eternity. I very much believe that, Eddie. But we do them gladly to save the others. Is it true what you said about David?"

I nodded dumbly.

"Tell me about it," he said.

Mullen said, "Don't believe him! He'll say anything to save his skin."

I said, "The gap in the dune."

Philbin nodded.

"The ocean came through it and smashed the cottage. David was in it. So was Cosgrove and Honor O'Toole. I saw the house go. No one could have gotten out."

Philbin nodded somberly. "Maybe it's for the best. He was too emotional for his own good. Poor David, he was brilliant in his own way. Too bad. We'll have a Mass said for him."

I said, "It was you and David who killed the gunsel Danny Dunn, wasn't it?"

"I'm afraid so. I've had second thoughts about that. Maybe the little feller wasn't as big a danger to us as we thought. But what's done is done. No sense crying about it, is there?"

"Did he use his machete?"

Philbin shrugged. "Maybe I shouldn't have let him. When he had that cutting thing in his hands, David was a changed man. Instead of the quiet lad that he was, he was the avenging angel, forever avenging his mother's murder. That blade was his manhood. I couldn't deny him."

Mullen sighed loudly and said, "Billy—"

Philbin said, "In good time, Hugh. Either the boat is still there, or it isn't. If it is, we'll use it and keep our rendezvous at sea. If it isn't, well, we'll find another way, that's all. The Coast Guard will be so busy inshore, there won't be a one in sight all those miles out. We have all the time in the world."

I said, "Did he use the machete to cut Max's wrists?"

Philbin smiled without humor. "Seems inappropriate, doesn't it? Like using a cannon to kill a mouse."

"You said you were going to hell. Is David going there, too?"

Philbin squirmed on his perch. "Possibly," he said. "Depends on whether he was sane or not. You called him crazy, and at this moment I'm inclined to hope that he was. As you know, Eddie, an insane person can't commit a mortal sin, because there can't be full consent of the will, not to mention sufficient reflection. So I would say no, David is not in danger of going to hell."

"Just you."

He nodded. "Just me."

"You were the one who tossed the grenade at Tom Costigan," I said.

I felt Alice's fingers dig into my arm. In my concentration on Philbin, I had almost forgotten she was there.

His eyes turned to her. "I'm sorry, Miss Costigan, it had to be done. Someone had to do it. You saw the papers your father had. Maybe they weren't enough to convict anyone, but they were almost certainly enough to prevent us from getting the atomic thing to the boys. That was the important thing. Our chance to throw out the English once and for all."

Alice said, "I would personally like to escort you to hell, Mr. Philbin."

He shook his head sadly. "I wish I could oblige, but I'm sure you won't be heading in that direction. You're one of the good ones, ma'am."

All Alice could do was gasp.

I said, "Why a grenade, for God's sake?"

Philbin smiled sourly. "I couldn't very well use the atomic thing, could I? A grenade seemed like the next best thing. Besides, we had a large store of them."

Alice said, "You're as crazy as your nephew."

Philbin braced his hands on his knees, apparently on the point of rising. He had a crooked smile on his face. "Keep telling me that often enough, and I might believe it," he said. "No, I am terribly sane, Miss Costigan. I have nominated myself the sacrificial black sheep who has taken on the sins of his compatriots, absolving them while condemning myself. We can't have a mass migration of Irish going to hell, now can we?"

Alice said, "That's Irish bull, and you know it."

"But it's a nice conceit, don't you think?"

He stood up.

I said, "What happened to your sister, Billy?"

He turned away from me, and I thought he wasn't going to answer, so I hastened to keep talking. "You said David's mother was murdered. She was your sister, wasn't she? What happened? Was she killed by the English? You're basically a man of peace—terribly sane, as you say—but it seems to me that when an otherwise rational man turns into an ideological terrorist, his claim of patriotism covers a deeper personal motive, revenge for some personal atrocity. Were you and your sister all that close, Billy? What happened?"

Brendan Power exclaimed, "Have you no sensibilities at all, man? Can't you see that the memories are painful?" He put his arm around Philbin. "Come on, Will. Forget the foul squawks of this turkey. We have a historic rendezvous to keep."

Philbin sat down wearily. "There's not much to tell, Eddie," he said, in answer to my question. "The Philbins had a pub in the wrong section of Belfast; they burned us out. But that's ancient history. My father came here and opened this pub. That was sixty years ago. Sixty years, think of that. I was born here, and so was Rita. We're native Americans.

"She was a fun-loving person, and very beautiful. Something like Honor O'Toole. That's why I liked Honor so much. When she was here, the whole pub lit up. And now she's gone, you say."

I shook my head sadly, on the verge of shedding sentimental tears for Honor O'Toole, who had lit up the pub for me, too.

Philbin continued in a monotone: "In any event, she married a young feller named Michael Glass, whose family came from Dublin. They were in the lace business, and they wore their Irishness like a badge. Like Brendan here. No offense, Brendan, but you're a professional Irishman. Nothing wrong with that. I just didn't get along very well with Michael, that's all.

"Anyway, they had a son, David, and when David was thirteen, that damned Dubliner took my lovely sister back to the old country for a visit. They left David with me. It was when the trouble in the North was starting in earnest.

"Well, Rita was aware of her own roots, and she talked that miserable husband of hers into taking her to the North—to Belfast—to see the site of the original Philbin's Pub. It was partly my fault, because I had gone there a few years earlier. But that was before the open warfare broke out.

"I told her there was nothing to see, just a damned English pub where Philbin's used to be, and the church of that feller Paisley at the end of the street. But Rita had to see for herself."

He rubbed his face with one of his large hands.

"I don't know the details," he went on. "But Rita must have decided that they should go into the English pub and toast a free Ireland with warm British ale. I knew Rita, and that's the sort of thing she would do."

After a moment of silence, he said, "That's where they were when the bomb went off."

He stopped talking.

I said, "That's it? A bomb went off?"

He gazed at me somberly.

"A bomb went off in an English pub? In Northern Ireland?"

He didn't respond.

"But . . . but doesn't that sound like it was set by the IRA? I mean, the English wouldn't bomb an English pub . . . would they?"

Mullen said, "It's time, Willie."

Philbin said, "Yes, it's time." He stood up with an air of finality.

"You don't understand, Eddie," he said to me. "It doesn't make any difference whose bomb it was. It wouldn't have gone off if the British army of occupation wasn't there. The whole Irish question is an English question. They've been there for centuries. It's long past time for them to leave."

"And the atom bomb is the answer to that?"

"Yes. An unanswerable answer."

I shook my head in puzzlement. The logic seemed to be that of another Englishman, Lewis Carroll.

"By the way, where is the bomb?" I asked.

A flicker of amusement showed in his eyes. "You're sitting on it," he said.

16

Suddenly I was aware of a tingling in my testicles, which zitted up through the abdomen to my stomach. I must have had a horrified look on my face, because Brendan Power laughed.

"Look at him, Will," he said. "The poor feller's afraid he's being unmanned by radiation. You'll never be able to father children, will you, Eddie? Your poor little tool is shriveling, and your stones are the size of BBs, and shrinking. Too bad you didn't get to use them, me boyo. Ah, the monastic life, it's too late now. Oh, my heart is bleeding!"

Mullen said, "What difference does it make, for God's sake? Let's get the hell out of here, and be done!"

With great exertion of willpower, I refrained from leaping to my feet. I remained seated on the smallish keg. "In here?" I said to Philbin. "I thought it would be larger." I rocked the keg tentatively. "And heavier."

Philbin took the handgun from the laughing poet. "You won't be needing this, Brendan," he said.

He turned to me. "We have to go now, Eddie. But just to satisfy your curiosity—and me not knowing any more about it than you do—it's a very crude device. The uranium in there doesn't weigh any more than five or six pounds. The weight comes from the metal framework that's keeping the two portions of uranium apart, and from the detonator."

"The detonator?" I said, unable to think, realizing that my time for talking was coming to an end, and we were entering the last phase—the time for dying.

Philbin said, "A small charge, Eddie. It fires a uranium bullet, so to speak, into a uranium receptacle, and—boom!"

"Forming a critical mass," I said.

"See," Philbin said. "You know as much about it as I do. Now, you and Miss Costigan have a choice. You will permit us to tie you up, or—"

"How do you set off the detonator?" I asked. "I mean, after all, nobody would want to be close enough to light a fuse..."

Philbin shook his head patiently. "You've done a good job of putting us off, Eddie. But there comes a time when we won't be put off. This is it. To answer your final question, the detonator is set off by this." He pulled a small black oblong from the pocket of his jacket.

"Remote control," I said. "How far away does—"

"Enough," Philbin said.

He held the gun in one hand and the remote control in the other. Suddenly he was the commander of his small army.

"Hugh, Brendan, move behind the two prisoners. Brendan, take the clothesline there. If they put their hands behind them, tie them. You can do that, can't you?... Hugh, if they don't do that, tap them on the head. Got it? Try not to fracture their skulls. I don't want you killing anybody, that's my job. Be careful, both of you."

The "hour of our death" had come, amen. Time for a last forlorn decision. Either permit ourselves to be immobilized for an ultimate death by drowning, or struggle with the two buffoons—who were now circling cautiously around to our rear—and force Philbin to shoot us while we tried to escape. I knew for a certainty that the hellbound barkeep wouldn't miss.

Alice clutched my hand. "I'm sorry, Eddie," she whispered.

I squeezed her hand and muttered, "Hang on."

I said to Philbin, "I'm going to stand up."

"Sit still!"

I stood up.

I said, "I'm going to bend over and pick up this keg."

Philbin said, "Hit him, Hugh!"

I raised the keg over my head and faced Hugh Mullen, who had started to spring toward me, and then froze. I towered over him.

I said, "It's heavy. I don't know how long I can hold it up there."

Philbin said, "Take it from him!"

The poet and the politician stood still, gazing fixedly at the keg loaded with death.

I said, "They don't know what would happen if it crashed on the cement floor, Billy. Was it you who moved it from the box to the keg? You ought to know how well it's cushioned against a jolt like that and going off accidentally. If it smashed on the floor, would your struts hold?"

"Most certainly," Philbin said. "Just put it down gently, lad."

I said, "If you're that sure, then you'd better shoot me, because that's the only way you're going to get this thing back—after it hits the floor."

The keg wasn't all that heavy, maybe sixty or seventy pounds, but in my weakened condition, I found myself wobbling under the burden. I hoped our captors wouldn't notice. Remembering my appearance, my matted hair and every-which-way whiskers, I hoped that all they saw was a wild man threatening to blow up midtown Manhattan if they tried to subdue me.

Philbin said, "I know you, Eddie. You wouldn't take a chance, even so small a chance, of incinerating a million people, women and children—your neighbors in Hell's Kitchen, Eddie—just to save two holy lives. Chances are, you and the lady will go directly to heaven. You're nauseatingly clean, the two of you. Now, just put it down like a good lad, and there'll be no hard feelings."

I thought that was very funny, so I laughed.

Philbin said in exasperation, "What do you *want*, man?"

Alice said, "I want to go to confession."

I looked at her in amazement.

She said to me, "This crazy man thinks we'll go directly to heaven. But first, I want to make sure. I want to go to confession. In Philadelphia."

I laughed, not sure whether she was joking or not.

Philbin swung back into his commanding voice. "Hugh, do what you're supposed to do; smash his ugly head. Brendan, you go for the keg. See that it doesn't hit the floor."

I was facing Hugh Mullen. He didn't stir.

I heard movement behind me, half turned, and saw Alice slug Brendan Power in the stomach. The poet doubled over and retreated. I swear what he said was, "Coo."

I said to Philbin, "It's hard to get good help these days, Billy. You're going to have to shoot me. And the deaths of those million women and children will be on your soul. You'll be deeper in hell, that's all. Go ahead."

Philbin said, "Okay, Eddie, we give up. Put the blasted thing down."

I felt like a statue of Atlas, holding up not the earth but the earth's antimatter. I knew he wasn't giving up. As soon as I relinquished the burden, we were doomed. By holding it aloft, I had produced a stalemate, which could last only as long as I had strength to keep it there. The ache in my shoulder and the weakness in my knees—and now a dizziness that was creeping up on me from below like an incoming tide—all told me that I couldn't do it for long.

I said, "I'll tell you what we're going to do, Billy. Alice and I are going to walk slowly to the staircase, and we're going to walk slowly up the stairs. And if you try to stop us, I'm going to drop this little old keg, and we'll see whether it goes off or not. What are the odds? Five to one? They're in your favor, Billy. Are you willing to play Irish roulette, with a million people as the victims? What do you say?"

Philbin said, "Eddie, as the Lord is my witness, if you try that, I'll plug you and take our chances. What do *you* say?"

I believed him. I looked around in desperation. Two guns were trained on me. I felt myself swaying. I saw the useless shillelagh on the ground behind Philbin. Alice was gazing at me, waiting.

Philbin said, "Put it down, like a good lad."

I did the only thing I could think of; I started to hum a tune, sounding even to myself like a demented person. The words I hummed were: "The same old shillelagh my father brought from Ireland."

Out of the corner of my eye, I saw Alice looking as dumbfounded as the others. Then I saw her nod, and heard her say, "Da would approve, Eddie. It was his song."

I don't think I ever felt happier in my life; I had the approval of Tom Costigan! I shouted, "Okay, then!"

Mullen said in bewilderment, "What *is* this—"

Facing Mullen, I said, "Catch!" And with my last remaining strength, I lobbed the keg to him.

For a fraction of a second, I thought he was so frozen in surprise that the keg would hit him and fall to the ground; and whether it exploded or not, Alice and I would have lost our last chance of staying alive.

Fortunately, Mullen's reflexes were still working. The keg hit him in the chest; he staggered back, dropped his gun, and held on to the keg with both hands. His momentum drove him to sit down—with the keg in his lap.

My reflexes were worse. I dove for the gun, slowly, clumsily. Philbin's first bullet hit me in the back. The pain was immediate and piercing. The second bullet hit me in the stomach. Then I had the gun, and rolled onto my side to point the gun and stop the awful fusillade before the patriotic pub owner could squeeze off the killing shot.

Alice's animal scream must have stayed the trigger finger, for the final shot never came. The shillelagh struck the side of Philbin's head with the force of a Hank Aaron home-run swing, and the horrifying sound of bursting bones was a crisp announcement that the self-condemned man was instantly and decidedly dead. The follow-through sent Philbin spinning against stacked cases of Jameson, toppling the top one to the ground amid the crackling of glass. The gun and the remote control device skidded across the floor.

Alice was staring at me, her lips pulled back in a snarl, the club hanging limply from her hand. To me, she was the reincarnation of an Amazon queen astride a field of carnage.

I heard soft wails coming from Brendan Power, and hoglike grunts from Hugh Mullen. I said, "The gun, Alice. Philbin's gun."

I coughed blood. The light was getting dimmer.

She saw the blood and started toward me.

I said, "Never mind about me. Call home. The police are there." When she hesitated, I said, "Go on. I'm okay."

She turned quickly toward the stairs.

"The gun," I said.

She said, "The remote control has a red light on it."

I said, "Don't touch it, for God's sake."

She took the gun with her.

I propped myself against a beer barrel and covered Philbin's two ridiculous henchmen with Mullen's gun. It was heavy in my hand and unsteady. I was bleeding badly, and slowly losing consciousness. A blind assessment of my wounds was that the bullet in the stomach had gone through blubber only, and, despite the sea of blood, was unimportant. The one in the chest was another matter.

Mullen and Power were talking to me, wheedling, waiting for me to pass out. I sent a bullet past them, and they shut up.

I glanced at the corpse of Billy Philbin. Fortunately, I couldn't see his head. He was the only one of the lot I had liked and respected, even knowing that he had planned to add Alice and myself to his list of murder victims. Like the Arab terrorists, he killed for a cause, but unlike them, he had no hope of reward in the afterlife. Being "terribly sane," he expected to go to eternal torment. He had nominated himself executioner to keep others from the same fate, using only an "innocent" nephew as helper, innocent by reason of insanity. I sensed that there was something terribly *insane* in his reasoning. On that basis, I prayed for him.

I kept myself conscious until I heard Alice coming back down the stairs. Then I let the darkness sweep over me.

17

I stayed in the hospital for two months, largely because my right lung refused to heal. The nearness of the police and the speed with which I was rushed to the hospital saved my life. In those first twenty-four hours I consumed more blood than Count Dracula on a hot night in Haiti. Alice stayed close to me without sleep until, during one of the transfusions, I told her a joke.

I hope my black humor will be forgiven, but when you're close to death and the blood of strangers is being siphoned into you—I swear one batch came from a wino, because afterwards I couldn't stop giggling—in those circumstances the only way you can keep the morbid fears from overwhelming you is by telling a joke.

I told Alice I heard it on the radio: Dracula had contracted AIDS and had voluntarily gone to Paris to have a wooden stake implanted in his heart.

Alice nodded wearily. "Sounds like you're going to live, Eddie," she said, and she went home to sleep.

And yet, I healed more quickly than Alice. We each had killed a human being, I with a screwdriver and she with a shillelagh, but I was more glib in quieting my conscience. I had done what had to be done to save primarily myself, secondarily Alice, and ultimately countless innocent people either in Belfast or London.

The same justification applied to her action, and she agreed with me that that was so. Whomping Billy Philbin was something she had to do, and there was no call for her to feel guilty. But there was an unthinking part of her that went into mourning, and grief continued to line her face even after I got out of the hospital.

Meanwhile, Hugh Mullen and Brendan Power plea-bargained, and were sentenced to five years in the prison at Ossining. The last I heard, the poet was happily constructing a new masterwork, "Ballad of Sing-Sing Gaol"; and I was sure that when he was released, he would be a big hit once again on the lecture circuit.

Alice slowly came out of her funk. She was too strong a person not to.

In the fall, we tracked down our whiskey priest at an upstate sanitarium. Father Frank, looking much older, was glad to see us. When we were leaving, he looked at my shoulder and said, "Flowers would be nice next time, Eddie."

"What flowers would you like?" I asked him.

"Bring Four Roses," he said, clearing his throat.

We promised to do that, but I suspect he will be disappointed when we give him real roses.

Alice rather primly referred to our visit as a corporal work of mercy.

Shortly after that, we were in my apartment having an after-theater drink. The play had been a romantic one, and we were in a romantic mood. I took her in my arms and kissed her. Her response was unusually passionate.

I said, "There's another work of mercy you must perform."

She stirred in my arms and gave me a quizzical look.

I groaned elaborately.

"Don't tell me," she said. "You're afflicted, right?"

Frankly, I didn't think she would do it, but in the succeeding hours she proceeded to comfort me with great zeal. Thereafter, we comforted each other with some regularity.

I shy away from reading the news from Northern Ireland. They're still killing each other over there. There's a terrible sanity in all this.